LOCKED GRAY /
GRAY /
/ LINKED
BLUE

Thank you so much
for attending the NJ launch!
Best wishes,

LOCKED GRAY / LINKED BLUE

STORIES

Kem Joy Ukwu

Kindred Books
Green Bay, Wisconsin

Locked Gray / Linked Blue is a work of fiction. Names, places, and incidents either are products of the author's imagination or are used fictitiously. Any resemblance to actual persons, living or dead, or locales is entirely coincidental.

The following stories previously appeared in other publications and are reprinted here with permission.
"Bars" in *Blue Lake Review* (August 2011)
"Demetrius" in *Carve Magazine* (Winter 2011)
"True, Perfect" in *Blackberry: A Magazine* (November 2012)
"Speakers & Headphones" in *TINGE Magazine* (Fall 2013)
"Proposed" in *Jabberwock Review* (Winter 2014)
"Text Me a Photo" in *PANK Magazine* (Spring 2014)
"Paying" in *Auburn Avenue* (November 2016, inaugural issue)

Published in the United States by Kindred Books, an imprint of Brain Mill Press.

Print ISBN 978-1-942083-97-9
EPUB ISBN 978-1-942083-99-3
MOBI ISBN 978-1-942083-98-6
PDF ISBN 978-1-948559-00-3

Cover design by Felicia Penza.

www.lockedgraylinkedblue.com

Contents

LOCKED

GRAY

LINKED

BLUE

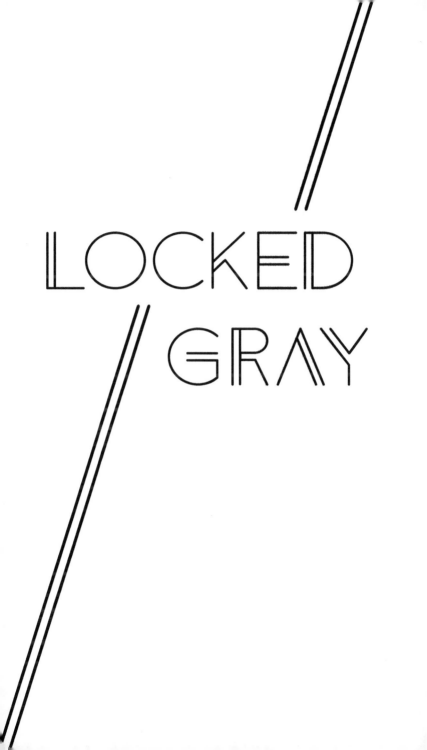

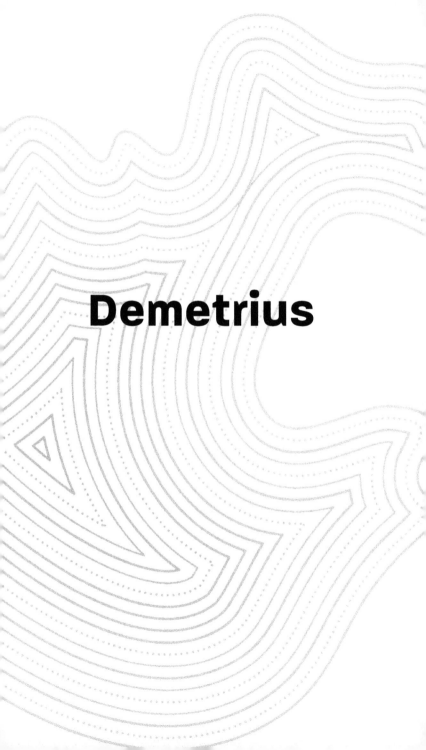

Demetrius

TURN TWENTY-FIVE TODAY. MY BIRTHDAY PARTY WILL START LATER THIS EVENING. IF MY MOTHER WERE HERE, THIS PARTY WOULD BE IN HER HONOR as well. I was born on her twenty-fifth birthday.

I was her gift, wrapped in blood and goo. It was the twenty-fifth of September when the nurse handed me to her. She held me, looked down at my face, and shook her head. That's how my older half-sister, Chioma, recalled it. She didn't tell me about her not wanting me. That part I figured on my own after I learned that my mother left my father, my half-sister, and me the next day with a written note that said, "I'm sorry," placed on top of ten thousand dollars in cash. The money was her gift to me. I have yet to spend it.

It currently sits in a savings account, collecting dust and interest. My father opened the account the following day after reading that note. Chioma told me that he sat in the living room on the green fake-leather couch we still own, reading that note for the first time as if it were one of his students' term papers. He sat on the couch for hours, Chioma insists, holding the crinkled white piece of good-bye with both hands.

"He wasted time with that note," Chioma said years ago to me. "Like he wasted time with that woman."

She sat down next to me on the same couch after we had returned from his service at the funeral parlor a few blocks away from St. Cornelius College, where he'd taught English. He wanted to be cremated. I insisted this to Chioma after she commented on the shame of the situation.

"The only reason he wanted to be cremated was because he knew there was no one back home to collect him properly."

According to Chioma, home was Nigeria. She was born and raised there. She referred to the fact that our father had no siblings, no parents, and therefore no aunties or uncles or cousins. He had his first set of in-laws, and then lost them when he married my mother only one month after Chioma's mother's death. The falling in love part with my mother happened before Chioma's mother passed away. That's how Chioma likes to remember it.

We sat there on the couch, talking. Chioma said something, and I countered. Chioma always wins. She has a beautiful talent with words. She uses them with the grace of an eagle and the ruthlessness of a dictator. She's an attorney.

"Things will be different now."

"How so?"

"Well, I had planned to move back to Lagos and live with Aunty Grace after graduation. That is no longer my plan. Someone needs to be here with you."

"I'm eighteen."

"And?"

"I'm old enough to take care of myself."

"Rubbish." One of Chioma's favorite words. "I have connections from Swade & Marks. I can surely land a position in their New York office after I graduate. That firm is not the best, but it will be suitable for me. In the meantime, you need to work on your college applications. You will apply to Cornell and NYU."

"I'm going to apply to St. Cornelius."

"Rubbish."

"You went there," I reminded her.

"A regret and error. The academic quality was substandard."

"I probably won't get into any other school."

"How have your grades been?"

"I am a proud B student."

"Daddy did not push you with your schoolwork?"

"My grades weren't everything to him."

"They should have been *something*. The first question Daddy always asked me, even before he greeted me, was, *How are your studies?*"

I didn't share this with Chioma—I don't think I ever will—but I knew why he asked her that question and why his first question to me was, *Did you eat?* He knew that she was, as they say, destined for greatness.

As for me, I didn't know what I was destined to do, who I was ordained to be. I still don't. And my father knew that I didn't know. I think he believed that I would never find the answer.

"You're good with school stuff," I noted.

"Well, you should be too. You need to figure out what you are going to do with your life, Obioma. I will not be here with you forever."

I knew that to be true. Seven years later, sitting here on this green couch waiting for my party to start, I know it now. My sister's family's luggage waits by our front door.

I REMEMBER CHIOMA'S WEDDING. THE CHURCH CEREMONY took place in Lagos. The event was a bright collage of yellows, purples, blues, and oranges showcased by long shirts and pants, dresses, and tall headscarves belittling gold and diamond crowns. It was the happiest day of Chioma's life. And, not-so-ironically, one of the saddest of mine.

I was one of her bridesmaids. It was a special honor to wear the dark purple sundress, she sternly lectured me in her Aunt Grace's dining area a few days before her wedding. She sipped her Earl Grey tea, looking through bridal magazines she'd brought from the States, even though she had finished her wedding planning long ago.

"When it is your turn, you will understand."

I laughed in response.

"Ah, that is right, no wedding for Obi. She will get married by a justice of the peace."

"It would be cheaper," I said. "More practical, don't you think?"

"More selfish. How could you do that? How could you not involve your family, your community?"

I shrugged and said no more. I stood, ninth in a line of ten bridesmaids and her matron of honor, looking over at her inside the church. As the sun shined on her through stained glass windows, I knew that I was losing her, even though she was never fully mine. I only had half her blood, and not even a quarter of her time.

Chioma has always been independent. Soon after I was born, she returned to Nigeria to live with one of her mother's four sisters. She attended a top-notch boarding school, staying with her Aunty Grace during vacation intervals, keeping in contact with our father by phone while he was here in the States raising me alone. She came back to the States once every couple of years to visit our father and me. She moved back here semipermanently to attend college at St. Cornelius, as our father wanted.

She often snickers about not choosing Cornell instead. That was one of the many sacrifices she made to be close to her family, she laments, moving to Westchester County instead of the land of Ivy. I know she chose St. Corn's because of the four-year, full-tuition scholarship she was awarded. Graduating from college debt-free, I'm certain, made the most sense to Chioma. Living close to us was a technicality.

After graduating summa cum laude in three years instead of the classic four, she moved to Ithaca to attend law school at Cornell, making up for her unforgivable error of passing it up for undergrad. She accomplished this feat almost all on her own, rarely asking our father for money, even though he was always ready to provide it.

Two months after our father passed, she agreed to marry Kenechukwu Agbochukwu, a fourth-year medical student at Johns Hopkins. They met through his parents, who are friends with Chioma's aunts. It only took a few months for her to accept that he was the one. He traveled from Baltimore to our father's service to support Chioma, which she appreciated.

I asked Chioma if she loved him the same day I received her bridesmaid lecture in her Aunty Grace's large estate in Lagos.

She said yes, of course.

"What about him do you love?"

"Sense," Chioma answered simply. "The man has it. Many men waste time. Ken does not."

Chioma was correct, Ken didn't waste time. He proposed to Chioma after knowing her for only a few months.

And there they were, the woman who gave up Cornell once and the man with lots of sense, exchanging vows before their God and three hundred of their closest family and friends.

Her matron of honor, Lynne Okocha, the only attendant Chioma selected to wear an evening gown instead of the sundress, told me during the packed reception that she was proud of *her* best friend for making such a wise selection, picking Ken to be her lifelong mate.

I wanted to pointedly reply to her, "I should be wearing your gown."

I DIDN'T REALIZE UNTIL A FEW DAYS AFTER THEIR wedding that I wasn't going to lose Chioma altogether just yet. She and Ken decided to move into our father's house. Both Chioma and Ken had finished their graduate education, and it would benefit them both to begin their respective careers in law and medicine in the States, specifically New York, where they could make connections that would serve them in the long run. And, most sensibly, they could live in our father's house in White Plains and save money by not having to pay rent. That was how Chioma explained it to me at the Murtala Muhammed Airport in Lagos, during her third day as Mrs. Dr. Ken Agbochukwu.

"It makes sense," she concluded before we said our good-byes.

I flew back to New York after that news and waited two weeks for Chioma and Ken to move in once they returned from their honeymoon in Italy. I geared up to start my college life at St. Corn's. They offered me a four-year, full-tuition scholarship to matriculate there (a sympathy token for my father's death, whereas Chioma earned hers from her academic achievements), and

I couldn't say no, which is what I explained to Chioma over the phone weeks before her wedding.

"Congratulations," she said. "Did you hear back from Cornell or NYU?"

"No," I lied. "Haven't heard yet."

"Call their admissions offices and follow up."

"I will," I said, knowing very well that I wouldn't. They had rejected me, which didn't hurt at all, as I only saw myself at St. Corn's. I couldn't lie further to say that I actually got in. She would have slapped me with her sandpaper palms if I had been accepted to either school and didn't go. I hoped she would forget eventually, with all her life-planning going on with Ken. But I knew better. Chioma forgets nothing.

We had one week of shared time after they returned from their honeymoon and before I moved half of my belongings to my dorm at St. Corn's to start my freshman year.

"You living there is pure rubbish, Obi," she said to me as I packed clothes in my bedroom. She stood against my door, folding her arms. "The campus is walking distance from here. What? You cannot walk to your classes?"

Of course I could have. I walked to campus at least every other day after our father passed, hoping to find him walking around, carrying his books by Márquez, Achebe, and Austen, wearing one of his colorful sweaters and New York Yankees cap. I wandered around the small campus for hours, believing that sooner or later I would catch him.

"Sure, I could. I could also walk to class from one of their dorms."

"You would save money by living here."

Save money or save sanity? I picked the latter. I zipped up our father's suitcase and hauled it out of the room, bypassing Chioma and her floral perfume. I walked down the stairs and encountered once again their boxes and luggage, reminders of the true reason I wanted to live far, far (all of ten minutes) away.

I knew I would stop by once or twice a month, not to say hello or to do laundry, but to show my face. To remind her that this house was also mine. To remind her that I existed.

CHIOMA HAS AN EYE FOR REDECORATION. SHE RARELY allows herself to watch television, she disdains the uselessness of it, but on the very few occasions she has turned on the flat-screen in the living room, the channel often has featured a show about home makeovers. She and Ken wanted to renovate the entire house to reflect their style. They started with their bedroom. Then the kitchen.

Our kitchen needed repair. Cracks decorated the tile floor, and the chipped white paint on the walls was friendly, always greeting me after entry. Chioma complained about these imperfections to my father during her visits when he was alive and then to me after he passed. It bothered her enough to offer snippy comments but not enough to do something about it. Until she got married.

I came to visit one weekend during my freshman year, entered the kitchen, and got lost.

"Welcome!" shouted the mahogany cabinets and granite countertops. The old appliances were now brand-new concoctions that looked too beautiful to be actually defined, let alone used. I tried to convince myself that I was standing in my house.

"Beautiful and clean. That is how everything should be," Chioma stated as she entered the kitchen behind me, startling me.

"It's quite lovely," I said. "How long did it take for you to do this?"

"Two weeks. It should have taken three, but we paid extra for less time."

"Very efficient."

"You know me well."

Chioma left. Still stunned, I also felt like I had won something without playing.

I decided to sleep over that evening, and after waking up the next morning, strolling down the stairs to the living room, my eyes caught a wall. I had never seen that blue wall bare. Dust and lint outlined the shape of a sofa. I paused, wondering who kidnapped our couch.

I continued my steps and eventually walked into euphoria, where Chioma and Ken were eating French toast and scrambled eggs on plates I had never seen before.

"Good morning, Obioma," Chioma greeted. Ken looked up from reading the *New York Times* and nodded in my direction, his usual hello.

There was a time I resented her calling me Obioma, my middle name. It means "good heart" in Igbo, Chioma's native language that I have yet to master (or learn). "Chioma" means "good God." Chioma has often joked to me that you can never have a good heart without a good God.

I have repeatedly wished that she would address me by my first name, Colleen. Over time, it has annoyed me less and less. I think it's because I'm grateful that she addresses me at all.

When I heard "Obioma" after not seeing our couch that morning, my heart didn't feel good at all.

"Where's the couch?"

"We gave it away this morning," Chioma answered, taking a sip of her orange juice. "It was too ugly to sell."

"Why did you do that?"

"Ken is going to renovate the living room."

My arms trembled. I wanted to grab her shoulders and shake her like salt over those perfectly assembled eggs on her unblemished flatware.

"I want it back."

"You want that old thing? What for?"

"Doesn't matter," I said. "You should've asked me first."

"Ken knows what would look good here."

My hand shot up, my pointer finger pointing at Chioma's doctor-man.

"This is not his home!"

Ken folded his newspaper. He stood up from his stool by the counter and walked out of the kitchen.

Chioma is the most beautiful when she looks like she wants to kill someone. Her dark chocolate skin and thick lips—gifts from her mother—look almost nothing like my face, with skin the color of cappuccino sprinkled with brown freckles—gifts, I assume, from mine.

The only features we share are our father's eyes—big, dark brown saucers. At that moment, they were paper-cutting me in two.

"What is his is mine, and what is mine is his," said Chioma, her voice low and even. How I wished she had yelled instead. I could have charged her next delivery to pure frustration, rather than an icy, numbing truth.

"If you had a husband, Obi, you would understand that."

She might have meant to say if I had someone. Any-one.

THE NEXT MORNING AFTER I SAID THE UN-SAY-ABLE in their new kitchen, I noticed the couch had returned. I knew it wasn't Chioma's doing. She doesn't believe in take-backs.

I thought Ken brought it back because I scared him with my *to-hell-with-you* statement. I think what I said, despite my callous release, made sense to him. He knew this house wasn't his place of permanence. It was just somewhere to live for the time needed. Why waste money on additional renovations when it was only a matter of time before they would move back to Nigeria? He probably wanted to thank me.

I entered the kitchen, where he sat by the counter on the same stool from the previous morning, reading the *New York Times* again, Sunday edition. He nodded toward me. I nodded back. I noticed there was no cup of coffee by him, so I decided to pour him some. I grabbed a Cornell mug from the brand-new cupboard and lifted the pot with already brewed coffee resting in it. I filled the mug slowly, wondering what he was thinking.

I placed my caffeinated apology on the counter next to him.

"I already had some, thank you," he said. "You can leave that for Chioma, she should be downstairs shortly."

I left the mug and walked out of their house, through the back door at the other end of the kitchen. I didn't want to see Chioma kiss her husband's cheek, ignoring the Cornell mug with steaming wake-up juice.

DURING THE SPRING SEMESTER OF MY SENIOR YEAR,

I called Chioma to wish her a happy birthday. It was then she told me she was five months pregnant.

"Twins. Boys. Such a blessing," Chioma said.

"Congratulations," I said. I'd had an idea she was expecting. Last time I saw her two months before, she looked a bit heavier and was annoyingly joyful.

"You are going to be an aunty of two. Praise God."

"Really, Chioma," I said, trying to pitch my voice higher. "That's wonderful."

"I do not know how this will affect my chances of making partner." It was Chioma's goal to move back to Nigeria as a full-fledged partner at her firm and start up an office there. Oil production and such, lots of opportunities, she said. She would make that firm global, she insisted.

"You do good work, I'm sure," I said.

"With twins, I will have to cut back in hours. Unless I find suitable daycare by the time they arrive."

"I don't have a job lined up yet. I can watch your babies until you make daycare arrangements."

Chioma waited a beat. "Thank you, Obi. That is a fantastic idea. Your help would be very much appreciated."

"My pleasure. Happy birthday," I said. I realize now why I offered my gift. Time is such a wonderful present. Its value is only noticed when it is gone.

On and off for almost three years, I cared for her sons. I wiped their bottoms and changed their diapers. I fed them, bathed them, soothed them, and taught them how to give high fives. Anytime Chioma or Ken was at work, building their careers, setting up bricks for their empires, I held down this half-renovated fort.

I loved it. Much to my own surprise, as I'm usually not a fan of children.

Except for a part-time babysitter who watched them while I worked at my part-time job at a local bookstore three days a week, I was here. I like to think that I left a mark on my nephews, but now I'm sure they'll forget me. I'll become a random note, lodged like a bookmark in between pages of a novel, there but not a part of the story.

Aunty Miscellaneous.

I try not to think of my nephews when they're not standing in front of me.

MY BIRTHDAY PARTY WILL START SOON. I REALIZE this after I look at the time on my outdated cell phone, one that doesn't have a camera and doesn't flip open. It's quite old, but I haven't yet found the desire to upgrade it.

Chioma's excited about this party. It was her idea, and she planned it. Invitees include Ken and the twins and a few of her friends from her days at St. Corn's.

My three close college friends are also on the invite list but can't attend. I don't take it personally, as all of them live far away. One's in Arizona, another lives in England, and the other lives in Philadelphia.

Chioma stressed to me that I should create a social networking page to help me keep in contact with them.

"It would be highly useful," she told me two months ago after she announced that she, Ken, and the twins were moving to Nigeria permanently.

We were in her kitchen. She manned the counter by the stove, preparing dinner. I sat by the kitchen island in the middle, flipping through a beauty magazine, pretending I wasn't fully present in the conversation.

"It will be a wonderful way for us to keep in touch. You would know everything that is going on with the boys, Ken, me," Chioma said as she chopped basil.

"Everyone else would know too," I countered.

"Yes. That is why it is efficient."

I remained silent, choosing to focus on the comforting, enticing smell of the stew she was preparing. The aroma, fresh and stout with onions, garlic, oregano, and curry, filled up the kitchen. I promised silently then that I'd tell her how much joy eating her stew has given me before she would leave for Nigeria.

Now, I don't know. Maybe I'll let her know online.

"I'm going to sign the house over to you," Chioma said, placing the cut pieces of basil in the pot. A declaration. As if she was going to pass on a mantle or a crown.

The house was already mine. Mine and hers, even though she believed the house became hers and Ken's. But now this house would be just my own. I should have had a celebratory thought about that. I didn't.

"When are you leaving?"

"We bought tickets for the twentieth, but we are changing our flights for the twenty-sixth."

"Why?"

"Do not be silly. We will not leave before your birthday," Chioma replied. "Actually, we are going to throw a party for you."

My next question was going to be a repeated "Why?" but I dropped it, not wanting to sound ungrateful.

I do feel grateful, sitting here in the living room, looking at the decorations. Purple balloons filled with helium, tied with white strings, float by the entryway into the kitchen and the stairs. My eyes make my way back to their luggage, waiting idly by the front door.

They'll leave tomorrow morning. I decide to leave now.

I stand up, grab my keys from the end table, and walk to the front door. My steps have always been light. That's why I don't worry that Chioma, Ken, and the twins, all upstairs, might hear me. They won't. And all's well.

I walk to St. Corn's. In late September, there is much buzz and restless activity on campus. The academic year has recently started, and students are walking about. Two students are throwing a football around on the main quad. Daylight is ending, and the sky is layered with stripes of orange and purple. The air is still warm, as if summer is a houseguest and doesn't want to leave quite yet.

I become jealous. It has been three years since I've graduated, and that should be enough time to get over that I'm no longer a student. I want to walk around here as if I still have options, possibilities, friends I see every day, an active social life, excitement about my future.

I remind myself that twenty-five is not old.

I walk to Crest Hall, my dormitory during my last two years there. It's also the building where a plaque was placed in the lobby honoring my father. He was a superstar of sorts here. His colleagues adored him. I knew this because many of them told me. As I walk, I now realize why he loved and needed this place. It loved and needed him first.

I wonder if he ever felt that way with anyone outside of here. I guess he hadn't. Maybe not even with me. Perhaps I had reminded him too much of my mother. I do share her first name. I never asked him why he named me after her. I never ask Chioma now that he's dead. Her response—I'm certain—would be, "Because the man did not have sense."

I wonder if I should be brave and ask her when I return home, just to see if I'm correct. I change my mind, knowing how she reacts whenever the topic of my mother comes up.

Chioma's mother was perfect. I know this from the large portrait of her that hangs on the wall above the stairway. Chioma placed it there after she and Ken moved in, along with photos of her aunts and cousins, pictures of Ken's immediate and extended family, and after they were born, photos of the boys.

Chioma's mother wears a red collared blouse in the picture. Her small, round afro caps her round head like a glove. Her red lips match her blouse. She is smiling. Not widely, just enough to show satisfaction. Just how Chioma smiles.

As I open the door to Crest Hall, I wonder if I should steal our father's plaque to hang it next to Chioma's mother. I decide against it as I see a security guard sitting behind a desk. He asks to see my student ID.

I balk. We never needed to show our IDs to the guards when I was a student.

"I just want to hang out in the main lounge, watch some television."

The guard waits.

"I'm alumni."

The guard shrugs.

I leave the dorm. As I'm walking, I think about my father. I think about Chioma. A realization overwhelms me. I know what I want to do. My decision is a surrendering but also a step—or leap—forward. As I reach the brick campus gates, I know where I'm going next. I hope I'm not too late and that their doors are still open.

It's one o'clock in the morning. I step inside the house, and the kitchen light is on. I walk toward the light, and much to my relief, no one is here. Just presents on top of the counter. I take Chioma's gift. I recognize it right away because it's the only box perfectly wrapped with purple ribbons. As I bring it upstairs with me, I notice their photos on the stairway wall are gone.

I WAKE UP. I LOOK OVER TO MY ALARM CLOCK. SIX fifteen. Their cab will arrive at ten. I close my eyes and nestle my head farther onto my pillow. I let Chioma believe that I'm in a deep slumber when she opens the door an hour later to check in on me. I wonder if she knows that I know that she has been doing that for years, at night and in the morning, opening my door slightly to see if I'm resting. I always hear the creak of the door, and even when I'm sleeping, it always wakes me. I always keep my eyes closed.

She closes my door. I hear her say to Ken, "Obi is still sleeping, I do not want to wake her."

"She knows that we are leaving today," Ken replies. "She should be up."

"She will rise soon," Chioma asserts. "She is not daft."

I hear my nephews squealing, being their jubilant selves. Their noises remind me of when Chioma and I discussed their names when she was eight months pregnant. It was the day after my graduation from St. Corn's. I was sitting on the couch, watching television. When Chioma sat down next to me, I immediately changed the channel to a show about first-time home-owners.

"Ken wants to give them English names," she said as she nestled her butt onto a cushion. "Matthew and Paul."

"They're also biblical names," I pointed out.

"Yes, they are. Well noted."

I nodded. After a few moments of silence, an idea landed in my mind, softly like a feather. This idea, I knew, was beautiful.

"Why don't you and Ken name one of them after Dad?"

"Dee-mee-tree-us," Chioma said, as if she were trying on the name like a pair of new jeans. Then came her verdict.

"I do not prefer it."

Matthew and Paul were born a month later. And three years later, they have grown into mini-men, with minds as strong as their mother's and whip-smart as their father's. They know how to read, how to use the toilet, and, of course, how to say no. Would they say no to their mother? No one says no to Chioma.

I would have broken that rule if she asked me to move with her to Nigeria when she first told me they were leaving. I would have said a long, drawn-out, humor-intended, "No."

She didn't ask. I didn't want her to. I wanted a threat instead. I had hoped she would order me with her voice, iced with a snarl, to pack my stuff and move with them.

She would have done so to Ken and her boys if they indicated in any way that they had no interest in moving. She would have done this rightfully so, for they belong with her. As I remove my comforter from my body and sit up on my bed, I allow myself to accept, like a failing grade, that I don't.

That doesn't matter, not anymore, because I have also allowed myself to accept that I still want to be close to them, even though they no longer need me or may never have needed me.

My hardwood floor is cold. My feet tell me they're unhappy as I stand up and walk over to my bedroom door. I open it, and Chioma stands there, waiting.

I expect a comment about last night. My disrespectful no-show. My rude absence.

"I prepared breakfast," Chioma says. "We will eat when you are ready."

I want to tell her what I did yesterday. Instead, I say, "Your stew is wonderful."

Chioma raises an eyebrow. "I did not make stew," she says. "I made eggs."

She turns around and walks down the stairs.

FIVE MINUTES TO TEN, AND THE CAB IS FULL OF THEIR luggage. Chioma and Ken decided not to take any of their new furniture with them. They, along with their sons, are moving to a house Ken's parents built for them in Abuja. The house is fully furnished, and there's no need to bring anything more than clothes and other essentials, Chioma told me some time ago. They'll travel to Lagos first to stay with her Aunty Grace for a month, and then they'll make their trek to Nigeria's capital.

I'm dressed with the clothes I had originally planned to wear for my party the night before, black pants and a dark green V-neck sweater with gold fringes on the sleeves. Black high-heeled shoes complete my ensemble. I'm ready for a party, but right now I'm not going anywhere but the front porch. I welcome this irony.

The boys are nestled in their car seats in the back of the yellow minivan cab. I choose not to hug them good-bye. I tell myself that I will see them very soon.

I wave to them and smile. I say, "Be good."

Ken stands by the cab. I really don't know what to say to him. I could say, "Take care of Chioma," but he already does that. Even "good-bye" seems disingenuous. All I say to him, as I stand on the porch and Chioma stands beside me, is "Good luck."

Another useless thing to say, he doesn't need it. Neither does his wife. I know this as I look at her. She turns to face me.

Her straight permed hair offers a contrast to my regal brown afro. I could share this observation with my sister, but I don't feel like it. I notice the air suddenly becoming cool. I place my hands in my pockets to warm them up. I recall yesterday's warm weather and wonder why Mother Nature made this change now instead of later today or tomorrow.

"I plan to wire five hundred dollars every month to your account, starting in October, when we're settled in Abuja," Chioma says to me.

"Why?"

"Do not ask me that rubbish question. It is not much, but hopefully with your income, it will suffice to assist you with bills and other expenses."

I want to tell her to keep her money, that I don't want it. But saying no wouldn't change anything. She'd do it anyway.

"The money will be wired to the bank with your first savings account," she says.

"I don't use that account."

"You will start."

I shrug and accept my defeat. I try to keep my mood light by admiring the green and orange leaves falling from the tree by our porch. Their varied shades are bright, vibrant, hopeful.

"Thanks."

"No gratitude is needed. It is the right thing to do."

Her face changes. She inhales and then exhales. Her cheeks perk up, and she smiles at me.

"I love you," she says.

I freeze. It's the first time she says it to me. She knows that I know this.

I relax my shoulders and return her smile. "I bought a ticket for a flight to Lagos leaving next week."

Chioma maintains her smile. "It would be fantastic to have you visit us."

I clear the fear dangling in my throat. "It's a one-way. I was thinking that I could live with you. Help you with the boys. Or I could move into an apartment close by. I would come back here eventually to sell the house, but living in Nigeria close to you would be good for me. Don't you think so?"

Chioma's face returns to the one I know. "No, I do not. It is not a smart idea. We will discuss it later. Call me."

I feel like scalding hot water has spilled on me. I offer no rebuttal.

Chioma turns and walks to the cab where Ken is standing, holding the door open to let her in. I watch Chioma step into the cab and seat herself next to her boys. Ken shuts the door and walks around to the front passenger seat. He gets in, shuts the door, and the cab drives off.

I turn around slowly to face my house. I enter it and close the door. I take off my shoes, and I walk to the living room. I see Chioma's wrapped gift sitting on my green monstrosity. I brought it downstairs earlier this morning, hoping I would open it in front of her.

I take the box and rip off its shiny wrapping. I open the box to find a phone, one that you can type with. One of those elite, fancy types. Also in the box are a charger and a manual. I nod and think to myself, she *is* efficient.

I still feel the burn from Chioma's last words to me, though it no longer hurts. It's as if this dulled pain is freeing me from something I never knew I was trapped in. I can't pinpoint the feeling, and I don't care to. I run with it.

I will go to the mall to have my present activated with my phone number. Before I do that, I will return to the copy center there to use one of their computers, perhaps the same one I used to purchase my flight yesterday after I left St. Cornelius. I will cancel my ticket.

I will then go to the furniture store. Using money from my never-touched savings account, I will redecorate this place—my home—and all the rooms in it.

Except the kitchen. I will leave it alone. If I never see my half-sister again, the perfect mahogany cabinets and shiny tiled floors will efficiently act in her place.

True, Perfect

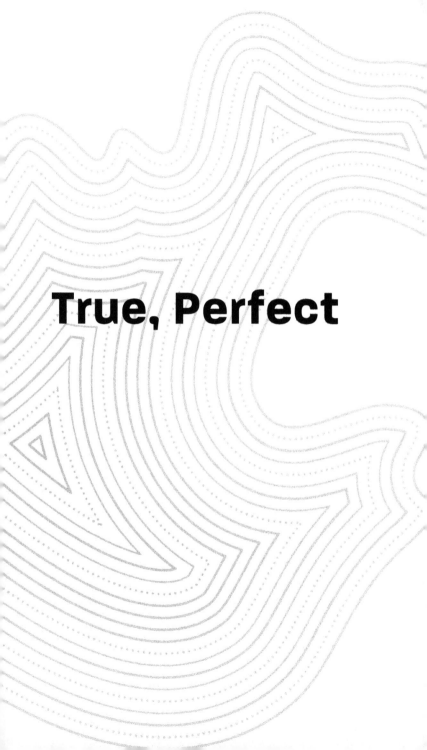

WE HAVE THE TALK. WE'RE SITTING ON YOUR LIVING ROOM FLOOR, FACING EACH OTHER, LISTENING TO AL GREEN ON your stereo. You say you want me in your life for good.

Saying *I want that too* would make you disappear. You scoot over closer to me and enfold me. Your arms are bars of brawn, and mine are wiry. Strong, like my faith in you, but thin, like my faith in *this*. You say the right words, do the right things, smell the right smells.

Even so, something is off. It's your perfection.

Perfect like your apartment. It's not your soft, suede couch that feels like I'm being hugged by feathers when I nap on it or your framed black-and-white photos of your favorite jazz musicians (who are also my favorites) hanging on your living room walls. Nor is it the bookshelf in your bedroom holding graphic novels featuring superheroes I knew and grew up with.

It's not the glass vase your grandmother gave you sitting on your coffee table that you fill with fresh red roses every Sunday since she died to honor her—I remember you told me during our second date that she thought red roses were nature's ambassadors of glamour. It's not any of those that makes your home perfect.

It's the top drawer in your dresser you cleared out for my clothes two weeks ago.

You did that without me ever asking you to, without prompts. You said that your home was mine and you wanted to be ready for when I would begin to believe that.

Your perfection is not in how you view the world—that it's a large, divided sphere where you believe people should help and encourage each other to make it less large, less divided. It's not in the loyalty you demonstrate every day to your family, your friends, and to me. It's not in how you smile or how you offer genuine laughs at my sorry attempts to show wit through mostly unfunny and unkind jokes.

It's in how you hold me.

In how you're holding me now. You make our embrace easy and natural, but terrifying. Like jumping on a trampoline or floating on an ocean without a boat nearby.

Fifteen years ago, my mother told me men like you existed after she learned my father left her.

"You see the good ones only in your sleep," she said.

She sat down on our kitchen floor, gripping her empty beer bottle like it was a rescuing hand pulling her up. She was tired—the long, weary life kind of exhausted. For years, I watched her try with futile effort to make the man who refused to marry her love her.

He is now married to another woman and has four

young children. I wonder what his wife had over my mother to compel him to make her legal.

Maybe she has what I have now that makes you want me the way you do.

Two months ago, I told my mother that I was seeing a wonderful man—smart, kind, family-oriented. And the winning trait—he loves me. The kind of love that never lets down.

She didn't believe me. She still doesn't.

I don't blame her.

On second thought, I do.

I blame my mother for wanting happiness from someone other than herself, for not seeing beauty, joy, and timelessness every time she sees her own reflection. I blame my father for spending empty years with her, only to check out when it was convenient for him. I blame you for wanting to revoke, revise, rewrite all of that.

I blame me for not letting you try.

I loosen my arms and kiss your cheek. You smell like rosewood, dark, sturdy, sweet. I inhale you like I'm taking one final breath. I get up off your floor and stand erect, as if I am a soldier ready to salute you, my head held up, my eyes looking forward. You are true, but my stance is false. I am not brave.

I turn to walk to your door, thanking God that I have my essentials—my car keys and wallet—in my back pocket. I say I'm going out for a walk.

You want to come with me. I ask you to stay here,

the weather's cold and I want you to stay warm. I hope you will always stay warm.

I tell you I will be back. You believe me.

Proposed

THE WATER BOILS. TOO SOON, OLIVE THINKS. SHE TURNS OFF THE STOVE AND WAITS FOR THE KETTLE TO STOP HISSING, SOUNDING LIKE a whistle letting her know that her time is up. Her time feels up, feels like stiff arms and legs, feels like a fatigue that only fully goes away when she sleeps.

Olive almost decides to turn the stove back on. Instead, she pours the steaming water into a mug and dips in a bag of herbal tea. She leaves it in and raises the mug up to her nose. She inhales its cinnamon smell.

Her friend, Wallace, waits in his living room. After a few moments, she hears him struggle to stand up from his leather recliner.

"Wait, Wallace," Olive says. "I'm coming."

Wallace obliges, resting again on his recliner as she leaves the kitchen with the mug of tea, blowing air on it. She walks into his living room and stands in front of him.

"You have an answer for me, Olive?"

Olive stirs the tea with her finger. She wants to withstand some heat, to feel something that she should be feeling from her friend's follow-up question to the question he had asked her seven minutes before. She looks at him and guesses that he most likely has not yet taken his medication.

"You sure you don't want tea?" Olive asks. "You can take your pills with it."

"Won't cure anything. Won't stop the inevitable."

"I know what's inevitable," Olive says. "My knees acting up if I don't take my medication."

Wallace sighs. "They'd act up anyway. Good night, Olive."

Olive looks down at the mug of tea, knowing that if she takes it with her, he will not say anything. She thinks he wants her to take it. So she would have a reason to come back. She returns to the kitchen and pours the tea out into the sink, the tea bag sticking inside the mug. She places the mug on the counter and leaves his kitchen. Without looking at him, Olive says, "Take your medication. With water, Wallace. Not rum."

She leaves his apartment to return to her own.

HER REMINDER THAT HER BODY IS NOT WHAT IT WAS thirty years ago comes with climbing the flights of stairs she takes from Wallace's apartment to hers. Her legs are achy from her rheumatoid arthritis. She pushes herself up and forward. Her determination to take the stairs has annoyed Wallace the few times he walked up with her from his apartment to hers.

"Never the elevator," she said to him one time after he complained. "This is good exercise."

"You just like doing things the hard way," Wallace said.

"You're lazy," Olive snapped.

"I'm smart," Wallace countered. "And elderly. Like you."

"Fifty-eight is nowhere near elderly. Screw you."

"I wish you would."

She couldn't do it with Wallace. She tried once. It was three years prior, one year into their friendship. They finished listening to one of his Sam Cooke albums, sitting in his living room, drinking rum and soda. Becoming tipsy after drinking three glasses, she thought to give it a try, thinking that he wouldn't mind. It had been five years since the last time she had sex. She wasn't sure how long it had been for him.

She kissed his cheek and placed her hand underneath his sweatshirt. She rubbed her hand on his chest, feeling long, wispy hairs. As she felt his dry and patchy skin, her instincts switched from unbuckling his belt to grabbing some lotion from his bathroom. Before she could get up from his sofa, he grabbed her shoulder and leaned in closer to kiss her. Olive jerked both her face and hand away.

"Sorry," Olive said. "Got ahead of myself there. Too much rum."

"No need to be sorry. Let's go to the bedroom."

"No," Olive said, sitting up from his sofa to move over to his recliner. "I was acting foolish. I don't want to sleep with you. I'm sorry."

"Now I am too," Wallace said. "I know you don't like me like that. Damn. Got me all excited."

Olive wanted to be excited too. She still wants that.

SHE ENTERS HER APARTMENT AND SURVEYS IT, THINK-ing about Wallace's question, as if her small space would help her decide. The open kitchenette is immediately to her left, and ahead of her is her living-room-by-day and bedroom-by-night. Her couch is her bed, her pillows serve as white decorative cushions. The only separate room is the bathroom, the only space in her apartment she feels good in, where she can pretend that beyond its door are more rooms.

She looks at a picture of her grandsons, Noah and Lionel, in a silver frame on top of her television set, re-membering how much she advocated to get just a photo.

"If I can't see them on a regular basis," she told her son, Geoffrey, their father, over the phone last year, "I'd like to see them on a daily one. On my wall or in my wallet. Something."

Geoffrey couldn't make the former happen. He didn't have primary custody of them, he still doesn't, and when he does have weekend visits with them, he can't fly them over to visit her because he doesn't earn enough to afford three airfares at one time. Olive lives in a different time zone, doesn't drive, and can't afford cross-country travel.

Olive has never reached out to her grandsons' mother,

her son's ex-girlfriend, out of pride and fear. Mostly fear. Olive wasn't kind to her when they were in acquaintance when she and her son were together. And thirty years prior, Olive was in the same position with her ex-husband's family, ready to curse out any of his relatives if they approached her claiming rights to a relationship with her son. She knows if she ever calls her grandsons' mother, she'd be timidly talking to karma instead.

Geoffrey's ex-girlfriend makes more money than him, and her new husband makes more than her. Four-year-old Noah and two-year-old Lionel don't lack of grandparent presence because the ex-girlfriend has two involved parents who live in the same neighborhood.

For Olive, this means there's no need for her to be around. And so, no leverage. This equates to two phone calls a month, one every other Saturday when Geoffrey has them. Every two weeks, she hopes her grandsons are in cooperative spirits to talk to a voice over the phone, knowing it doesn't contend with seeing their other grandmother every other day when she babysits them. Olive knows this from Noah's reports of their fun afternoons with their "Gramma," how she lets them eat ice cream and watch cartoons before dinner.

"I don't care about that," Olive has wanted to snap at Noah anytime he would mention her, but she has never and can never, because she has to care, she has no choice. She would nod and say, "That's nice. Nice of Gramma." Olive would talk to Lionel and he'd volley the conversation with a few marbled words or a random exclamation befitting two years of age. She often prefers this over Noah's coherent sentences about his Gramma. She looks forward to Noah starting kindergarten next year, when he will have other things to tell her that won't involve her dessert-and-TV-before-dinner counterpart.

In between their biweekly phone calls, she talks to their faces on top of her television. She sometimes asks how their days were and lectures them about various things. They only respond with wide-toothed smiles.

"Noah, open up my mail. Tell me where they're from," Olive orders her older grandson. "If it's a bill, throw it out."

Olive can no longer ignore the large stack of unopened mail resting on her couch. If Noah were there, he would throw out almost all the envelopes. Half of them are overdue medical bills. Only two envelopes are bills that she can afford to pay this month.

When she returned to her building earlier that evening from her part-time housekeeping job on the other side of town, she opened her mailbox in the lobby. She saw two additional white envelopes, one from the physical therapy center that helped her recover from her ankle operation and another regarding one of her three maxed-out credit cards. She placed them back inside her mailbox. She took the stairs straight to Wallace's apartment on the second floor, knowing that if she returned to her studio on the fourth floor first she would have ripped up the other envelopes waiting for her. She would have thrown the torn pieces in the air, all of them falling around her like confetti.

She hoped seeing Wallace would remind her of her blessings. That she had a friend. That her friend was likely more depressed than she. That she could help him. She would cook him dinner and they would eat together. She would forget about her bills while eating rice, sautéed chicken and green peppers, listening to Wallace's complaint-of-the-hour.

Once she opened his door with her own set of keys, she heard Sam Cooke's voice. The same song that played when she threw herself at Wallace a few years back. She broke down in tears.

"What the hell is wrong with you?" Wallace asked, leaning forward from his recliner.

Olive wiped her eyes with the back of her hand. "No matter."

"Well, can't be PMS. You're well past that."

"Screw you."

Wallace leaned back on his recliner and chuckled. "Still waiting on that."

Olive closed the door and sat on his leather sofa. She told him about the bills. She told him about the additional therapy she needed that her subsidized insurance wouldn't cover. She told him about how the cost of her medication had increased. She told him how she felt pain in her ankle, the surgically fixed one.

She told him how she felt the most pain from kneeling down on Gertrude Brimmey's bathroom floor to wipe off grime around its tiles. Her rheumatoid arthritis flaring up in her arms and legs to ask, *Can I help?*

After she was done, her tears had dried. She stood up to walk to his kitchen, feeling composed enough to cook dinner. Before she took her first step, Wallace spoke.

"There's a solution for all that."

He proposed his idea, ending it with a question.

"I'm going to make some tea," Olive said.

SHE TURNS HER CELL PHONE ON AND HEARS IT BEEP. She often leaves her phone at home, not being used to receiving phone calls. The person who would call her most lives two floors down and doesn't own a cell phone. She hears that she has two voicemails.

The first one: "This message is for Miss Olive Armnion. My name is Verita Nolan, Human Resources Manager at Stainless-N-Spotless Cleaning Group. We received your resume for our administrative assistant position and would like for you to come in for an interview this week, as we're looking to hire someone before the holidays begin. We have a slot this Friday at 2 p.m. I will call you tomorrow to confirm your interest and availability. Thank you."

Olive drops to her knees. She presses a button on her phone to hear the message again. She listens to it three times more. She doesn't feel any aches from kneeling. She listens to it one more time. She shrills.

They worked. The classes at her local library that taught her how to use a computer. The workshops there that showed her how to create a resume. Knowing that her body would no longer allow her to enjoyably work as a full-time housekeeper, nanny, and caretaker, she needed work that would be easier on her limbs and joints.

A year ago, Geoffrey suggested she look for an administrative position, being able to sit down in one place and work instead of standing, carrying, kneeling, bending, scrubbing.

She noticed the help-wanted ads in local newspapers wane over the years until one day the classifieds no longer had them. The Internet, Geoffrey informed her, had become the key to everything. She asked Wallace for his help, to which he responded, "The Internet is the devil." If you're determined to become evil, he continued, go to the library to learn and practice.

Olive became acquainted with things cyber at the local branch. She learned how to create electronic documents and set up an e-mail account. She learned how to use Internet search engines to look for positions. She read books about writing cover letters.

She called one of her former employers, Stella Madney, for advice after her ankle surgery. They grew up together, kind acquaintances more than close friends. Olive admired Stella's successful, money-making, benefits-carrying career. She was a human resources director who paid Olive to take care of her elderly mother for five years until she died at ninety-six.

"I should warn you, Olive, it's cutthroat out there now. Don't quote me on this, but it won't be easy for you to make a career change, in this economy, at your age," Stella told her as if she were giving her permanent bad news. "You're going to be competing with hundreds of people who are more educated, more experienced, and much younger than you."

Olive asked her to elaborate on the age part.

"Younger people, Olive. Recent graduates. Those who may be willing to work more for less. Again, don't quote me on this. Companies hire people of all ages, but it's about your whole portfolio, everything you have to offer. Like your education. You have a high school degree, but there will be candidates applying for entry-level positions with master's degrees. That kind of thing. I don't want you to be surprised. I wish I could connect you with a position here, but I can't. The best thing for you is to apply for positions that are similar to what you're doing now."

I don't care about surprises, she wanted to say to her former employer. I need this. I can do anything. Anything and everything just as well as everybody more educated or more experienced than me and anybody younger than me.

"I need more pay and benefits, Stella."

"I understand. Put me down as a reference. You know

I'll give you a sterling one. Mama wouldn't have enjoyed her last years if it weren't for you."

Olive nodded, agreeing with her.

"And by the way," Stella added. "Do you still keep your hair in cornrows?"

"Yes."

"Take those out before any interview."

"I've seen you go to work with cornrows, afros …"

"After I got the job. *After.*"

Olive understood, resenting her advice.

"Don't forget to put me on your list. I'll let the whole world know how fantastic you are."

Because I am, Olive confirmed to herself as she added Stella Madney to her list of references. She spent hours submitting applications to administrative positions, both part-time and full-time. Over two hundred in the past six months. She would have applied to more, but she could only use the time the library allotted her. One hour per day.

Six months of no responses, no feedback, no *Thank you, but.* Until this evening.

As she stands up, she listens to her next voicemail. "It's me. I want to take you out tonight. I'll be around to pick you up at eight."

Isaiah. She calls him back, and he answers.

"Hey. I assume you got my message. I'll pick you up."

"Who said I was home and free?"

"You're not both?" Isaiah asked.

Olive thinks she should say no. In the nine months

that she has known him, he has not yet seen her place. She invited him over several times, but each time he insisted on spending time at his house.

"More room," he said once to her after he took her to see a movie, one month into their undefined relationship.

"How would you know?"

"You said you live in a small one-bedroom."

With a snort, Olive retorted, "I never said I had a bedroom. I live in a studio, and I'm not asking you to move in."

"I have a king-size bed," Isaiah countered with a wink. That cursed wink. Magical—as if he had sprinkled crystal-lighted dust on her face to make her irritation disappear.

"Screw you," she almost snapped at him. Instead, she did it, in his one-story house in the wooded, suburban part of town.

"So, am I getting you or not?"

Olive wants to sound annoyed, maybe even detached, but she can't. She has an interview. And now hope. She wants to keep her light, airy feeling of possibility going.

That feeling is interrupted with a quick thought of Wallace. She thinks she should have made dinner for him, instead of switching gears to tea. Wallace didn't want tea. He wanted her answer.

"Yes." An answer she could give easily, quickly. "I'll be ready in twenty minutes."

"I'll be downstairs in an hour with a surprise for you."

Olive shuts her cell phone and smiles. A surprise. Earlier that evening in Wallace's apartment, she was bills and tears. Now she is voicemails and optimism. She listens to Verita Nolan's voicemail again. Then she chucks her cell phone at the stack of envelopes on her sofa. They fly and skip like bowling pins. Strike.

OLIVE EXITS HER APARTMENT BUILDING CAREFULLY, lightly tapping the ground with one foot to see if it's icy. It had snowed and rained earlier that evening, just when Olive first returned home for the day. She feels secure enough to steadily walk outside of her apartment building's grounds, where, by its entrance, a car waits on the street. The car honks.

A front window rolls down. It's Isaiah. "What do you think?"

Olive doesn't recognize his car. It's brand-new, she can tell from the shiny symbol on the tip of its hood. She approaches the car and leans down slowly to fully capture his face, mainly his smile. She knows his widening smile comes from her seeing his car, more than him seeing her, but she's okay with that.

"I don't think this surprise is for me," she says.

"Just got it this afternoon," he says. "Get in already. Let's drive somewhere."

"I thought you were taking me to your house."

"We'll go there eventually. I want to drive us someplace where we can fool around."

Olive enters his car, the smell of leather whiffing through her nose. She turns to look at the pristine backseat. She knows that her legs are not what they were thirty years back, pre–rheumatoid arthritis. She would not be as flexible as the younger women who flirt with Isaiah at the gym he owns. Olive can see any of those ladies stretching their toned limbs painlessly in the right places in his backseat. She knows that he dates a couple of them, he doesn't hide it. It would only be a matter of time before he would break in the leather back there with some younger lady's backside.

It might as well be hers.

A lay in his new car. She won't be his last, but she'll be his first. Take that, she thinks, she smirks, picturing Belinda, one of the sweaty, sports-bra-wearing twenty-five-year-old girls who works out at Isaiah's gym, dating him on the side. She sees tall Belinda and her legs of shiny brown iron standing on the corner, beaming at Isaiah's luxury car, only to scorn at Olive's face when she would roll down her side window. Olive lowers the window, hoping that Belinda will appear on the sidewalk.

"All right," Olive says.

Isaiah drives them away, and Olive turns on his radio, tuning it to a station playing Luther Vandross. She looks around the interior, admiring how clean and new everything is. She sees Isaiah's satisfied smile and wants to be its cause. She wants to meld her back and butt onto the leather seat, melting into it, as if to disappear to become a part of it.

It's one thing that Isaiah is classically handsome, the fine wine kind of good-looking, with distinguishing gray specks in his hair, symmetrical features, his muscled body with a brown shade belying his sixty years and pink lips that Olive pretends are tasty gobs of bubble gum when she kisses them.

It's another that he knows it, owns it, and shows it off. It bothers her at times, his cocky confidence. But it doesn't override her infatuation. Olive not only wants to be with him but also wants to become him. Financially secure, physically sound, emotionally independent.

She thinks she may never become those things. She thinks all she can be for now, especially this evening, is painfully flexible.

OLIVE WAKES UP, AND ISAIAH IS GONE. MAKES SENSE, she thinks, he opens his gym early in the morning, around six. She looks at his clock on his nightstand. It's seven, and she has to be at Gertrude's at nine. Gertrude Brimmey is one of her customers. Any other person would call Gertrude her boss, but that would mean something else. Olive prefers the term *customer*. It means that Olive has a choice about taking two buses to Gertrude's three-story home on the other side of the city, not far from where Isaiah resides. *Customer* means that Olive can drop her work for Gertrude anytime. That's what she tells Wallace and Isaiah when she leaves either man's company for work: "Time to meet my customer."

Olive rises out of Isaiah's bed and walks to his bathroom. She looks at herself in the mirror and notices that her cornrows are frizzing out a bit. She takes petroleum jelly from his medicine cabinet and slathers some on her braids to smooth them down. She douses her mouth with water, gargles, and spits. She sees two toothbrushes, and one of them, she knows, is not Isaiah's. She deduces that his last visitor most likely left her toothbrush there on purpose. Belinda? Perhaps Lynnette, one of the trainers at his gym.

Olive is tempted to throw it away in his wastebin, but she reminds herself that she's a lady. Instead she places it in the sink, a harmless oops. She washes her face, leaving the toothbrush there to catch the falling liquid. Another oops.

She places the toothbrush back into its holder and dries her face with his hand towel. She looks at her face in the mirror, a bit satisfied that her hair looks somewhat presentable. She sees her cocoa-brown face, decorated with slight wrinkles and darker brown spots. The wrinkles Olive doesn't mind. The spots are her problem. She couldn't have prevented the wrinkles.

She wants the spots to go away. She usually rubs on drugstore makeup to cover them. A three-dollar concealer that doesn't last more than three hours. She didn't bring her plastic makeup bag with her on her date with Isaiah, she didn't anticipate sleeping over at his home, thinking that he would have driven her back to her apartment building the same evening. She thinks she won't look her best when she arrives at Gertrude's house. She wishes she had a toothbrush to leave in Isaiah's bathroom. She snickers at herself for not being prepared.

It only takes a ten-minute bus ride for Olive to get to Gertrude's from Isaiah's. Olive enjoys the short bus ride. She sees the houses become larger and the properties greener as the bus travels down two roads to reach Gertrude's house.

Gertrude Brimmey's house looks like one Olive has dreamed of living and dying in. Out of all the houses Olive has cleaned in the past forty years, Gertrude's home is the largest and most stunning.

Gertrude came from modest beginnings and married into money. That was the first thing she said to Olive after she arrived at her home when she first started working for her six months earlier.

"This house isn't me, I tell you," Gertrude continued, escorting her into the kitchen. Olive disagreed. Gertrude seemed to fit into the scenery of her home, her brown bouffant hair, her bright green eyes and gold jewelry meshed with the cream walls. It can be me anytime, Olive almost replied, looking past Gertrude's elaborate kitchen, which opened up to her wide living room, realizing that the space was larger than her entire studio. She admired the rustic designs of the furniture and how the hardwood floors spoke of age but never creaked when stepped on.

"My ex-husband bought this house before we got married. Three decades later, he asks for a divorce. Give me my freedom quietly and I'll give you the house, he said. Really? I thought he already gave me the house, you know? I thought it was already mine as his wife. But it was his during our entire marriage. He bought it with his money, my name was never on the deed. What a bastard."

Caught off guard by her candor, Olive said, "My ex-husband was a bastard too. But he never gave me a house."

She regretted saying that after seeing Gertrude's eyes popping widely, her smile extending, as if Olive had just offered an invitation of friendship by sharing that tidbit. She tried to regain her stern facial expression, as she didn't want Gertrude to speak. Her house was speaking for her. It spoke to Olive, whispered to her, shouted, sang.

"The rooms that need the most work are the bathrooms and the kitchen. I know I only have you for four hours, but I hear you can make magic in minutes. The agency told me that you're the best."

Olive lifted her chin slightly. "Where are your supplies?"

Gertrude led her to the kitchen and pointed to a closet door by the backyard entrance. "Everything's there. If you finish early, we can have a drink."

"If I finish early, I leave."

"I paid for four hours," Gertrude said, smiling wide. "If you finish in three, I still can keep you here for one. Besides, I want to hear more about your ex. We can compare notes."

Olive narrowed her eyes and turned toward the supply closet.

"I'm going to get started now."

"I can't talk to you while you're working, the agency told me that too, they said that you love to work in silence," Gertrude said, laughing. "I'll leave you alone until you've finished. Then two glasses of white wine await us."

Olive grabbed a bucket with bottles, sponges, gloves, and towels. She shut the door as if to say shut up.

"Thank you in advance. I only drink red."

Six months later, she and Gertrude now drink brandy. After Olive cleans her bathrooms, kitchen, and the rest of her house, she sits with Gertrude in her dining room. Olive listens about Gertrude's dating life. Her three children and five grandchildren. Her ex-husband and his current wife. Olive talks about her grandsons, inventing stories about making visits to see them.

Today, after she finishes her work, she talks about yesterday. She leaves out her breakdown about her finances, fearing that Gertrude wouldn't understand, or, worse, that she wouldn't care. Olive tends to do this during their conversations, apple-picking things to share, picking those fresh enough for both of them to eat and digest.

"I was proposed to," Olive says, sipping her brandy, looking as if she has just laid out a problem for Gertrude to solve.

"That's great," Gertrude says slowly. "I didn't know you were seeing someone."

"I am," Olive confirms, exhaling. "His name is Isaiah."

"Congratulations," Gertrude says as she raises her glass, offering a smile. "Did you say yes?"

"No. I haven't given him an answer yet. And Isaiah is not the one who proposed. My friend did."

"Are you two ... is he a friend with benefits?"

"The kind that can afford enough medical attention," Olive doesn't say. She knows that is not what Gertrude means.

"No," Olive replies.

"What I wouldn't give to have a man get down on his two knees to ask me for my hand in marriage," Gertrude says before gulping down the rest of her brandy.

"Two knees? Isn't it on one?"

"My ex-husband proposed to me on one knee. Next time, I want two. Lets me know that he really, really wants me. Or desperately needs me. I prefer both, but I'll take either." Gertrude laughs.

Olive nods her head. She knows Gertrude would marry again so she would no longer be lonely. Olive realizes that she herself would marry again so she would no longer be alone.

Gertrude's laughter stops after she looks at Olive's left hand. "I know why you haven't made up your mind yet," she blurts out.

"Because I don't love him?"

"Forget love," Gertrude replies, laughing again. "How was the ring?"

OLIVE ARRIVES BACK TO HER APARTMENT BUILDING and ignores her mailbox. She reaches the staircase and stops. She isn't ready to stop by Wallace's apartment. She doesn't want to see his door only to walk past it to the next flight of stairs. She turns around and takes the elevator.

As she reaches her apartment door, she wonders if Wallace took his medication. She also remembers it is Thursday. On late afternoons every other Thursday, she washes Wallace's clothes. On Mondays, she picks up his groceries. On Sundays, she sits with him all day, listening to his albums, sometimes cooking him a big meal with leftovers for the week. He offered one time to pay for her services years ago, but she refused. It was the kindest thing she remembered saying to anyone in years: "You're my friend. I don't mind taking care of you. At no cost."

Olive still doesn't mind. She thinks she should go downstairs. She shakes her head and enters her apartment. She sees the mess from the bills splattered all over her floor by her couch from yesterday and refuses to clear it, a rarity.

"Leave the envelopes on the floor," she orders Noah. "Don't touch them. Let them fester."

She heads over to the wooden stand-up closet adjacent to her television, stepping on envelopes as she reaches it. She sees the suit that she delayed paying one of her hospital bills for. A black blazer and matching pants she purchased from her favorite department store when she first started looking for an administrative job. She also takes out the pearls that Geoffrey bought for her on behalf of Noah and Lionel last Christmas. One necklace and matching earrings. These are what she will wear tomorrow, when she convinces Miss Verita Nolan that she is the person she should hire.

Olive nods her head and touches her thick cornrows. Recalling Stella's advice, she sulks, walking over to her favorite room to comb them out.

The Stainless-N-Spotless Cleaning Group's main office smells like a mixture of fresh linen and lemon. As Olive sits outside of Verita Nolan's office, she thinks about Wallace. She regrets not washing his clothes for the week. He has enough clean underwear and pants to last two more weeks. If he still smoked cigarettes, she would have done his laundry, but since he quit a few months after they first met, she knows his apartment will manage in terms of smell. Not like Wallace would be bothered by the funk of his own clothes in the hamper in his bathroom. It would merely bother the only person who visits him.

She sits next to a young woman who would look like her daughter if she had one. She wears a navy blue business suit with pointy black heels. Her natural black hair is short and cropped to fit her square-shaped face. She wears eyeglasses without rims. She turns to face Olive just as Olive realizes that she has been looking at her younger look-alike for a bit too long.

"Hi," the young lady says.

"I was admiring your suit," Olive explains.

The lady smiles wide. Straight, aligned white teeth, Olive notices.

"Graduation present from my mother," the lady says, stretching out one arm, showing off the fabric.

"Congratulations. From college, right? That's good. Good for you," Olive says, offering a genuine smile.

"Graduate school, actually," the lady clarifies, adjusting her glasses. "I finished back in May. I earned a master's degree in hospitality and tourism."

Olive nods, her smile now feeling plastered on. She turns her face away and stares ahead.

"My mom bought this suit as my gift, when all I really wanted was a new laptop. She figured a suit would be more useful. And it has been. This is my eighth interview with this outfit."

"Eighth?"

"I'm lucky. I know people who have been looking for over a year who have been only called for one. My brother got a call for an interview yesterday, and we took him out to dinner to celebrate. He's been out of work for two years now," the lady says, shaking her head. She turns her face to Olive's. "Love your pearls."

"Gifts from my grandsons."

A tall woman wearing the same pearls as Olive and the same shoes as the recent graduate steps outside of her office.

"Olive Armnion?"

"Yes."

"Verita Nolan. Thanks for coming. If you would follow me," Verita Nolan says.

Olive clenches her jaw, feeling pain in her ankle as she stands. She is wearing her round-toe, short-heeled shoes instead of her orthopedic sneakers. She doesn't wince, doesn't limp. She walks straight and aches.

VERITA NOLAN'S OFFICE IS SMALL AND ORDERLY. Stacks of folders rest on her wooden desk. Olive sits down on the chair in front of her desk, facing her.

"Why do you want to become our administrative assistant?"

"I love the work I do and have done," Olive begins as she folds her hands on her lap. "At the same time, I would love an opportunity to broaden my experience. I believe that I would easily transfer my domestic organizational skills to your office. I love order and would make sure that your office is managed efficiently." Olive nods. She's happy with what she says, how her voice sounds, how she imagines herself looking to Verita Nolan.

"You do not have administrative experience listed on your resume," Verita Nolan says.

"I'm a fast learner."

Verita Nolan sets Olive's resume aside on her desk. "Stainless-N-Spotless Group is expanding, even with the economy. I know you're here for the assistant job, but we're also looking for more housekeepers. Your resume is perfect for one of our openings. If you're interested, I have one that is full-time and live-in."

Olive responds with a smile, a fake one.

"Does it include benefits?"

"No, but the pay is on rate with other agencies."

Olive's smile is still fake. She hopes Verita Nolan can't tell.

SHE RETURNS TO HER STUDIO AND RESTS HER BLACK handbag on her kitchenette's counter. She sees the envelopes on the floor and relents to picking them up. She places them in an even pile against her couch. She takes one off the top and opens it.

It's her bill from her ankle surgery. $4,158 in total she still has left to pay. She pays $50 every other month so they won't call collections on her. If they do, she figures they won't have much to collect.

She sets it aside and reaches for the next envelope. Before she touches it, she hears her cell phone buzz. She rushes to her handbag and retrieves her phone. She flips it open and smiles at the name she sees.

"Isaiah."

"Hey, Olive. What are your plans for Christmas?"

Usually she visits with Wallace. Last two Christmases, she prepared a small turkey and cooked vegetables for both of them in his apartment.

"What do you have in mind?"

"My daughter invited me over to her apartment. She wants me to bring a guest."

Olive has never met Isaiah's daughter before. She knows that she's in her late twenties and has a two-year-old daughter. Olive has never seen Isaiah in his grandfather element. She thinks about the other women he sees. The ones around his daughter's age.

"Why don't you ask one of your other lady friends?" Olive inquires, already knowing the answer. She's probably the most acceptable option to his daughter, the most age-friendly.

When Isaiah doesn't respond, she says, "I'll come only if you come get me. They say it may snow next week, and I'm not about to take a bus in that weather."

"I'll pick you up."

Olive hears her doorbell ring. "I'll call you back," Olive says before shutting her phone. She walks over to her front door. She opens it and sees Wallace standing there with his gray cane, wearing his gray sweat suit and black sneakers.

"What are you doing here?"

Wallace shrugs. "Good question. Good suit. Did you get a new job? Looks like you just started one."

"Just an interview. Let's talk about it later. I'm tired."

"Fine, see you next week. Perhaps you'll give me your answer by then."

"Next week? You mean Christmas?"

"Are you going to see Geoffrey?"

"No."

"I suppose you'll be coming over then."

"I just made plans, I won't be stopping by. Maybe you should call Harold," Olive says. Harold is Wallace's estranged brother, his only sibling.

"You know better than to suggest that," Wallace says.

Olive nods. Wallace and Harold haven't spoken in fifteen years. They've been estranged ever since Wallace told Harold's wife that she was inept to her face in front of Harold during their mother's funeral. Wallace hasn't apologized and will never. It was the truth, he always said to Olive whenever the memory came into conversation—his ironclad, permanent defense.

She shrugs. "He's your family. That won't change."

"Merry Christmas in advance then," Wallace says, dropping his gaze from Olive's face to the floor, turning to walk toward the elevator. Olive watches Wallace's slow gait supported by his gray cane. She winces.

Olive shuts her door quickly. She looks at her cell phone next to her rebuilt stack of bills instead. She takes her cell phone and skulks off to the bathroom. She sits on top of the closed toilet seat and closes the door.

She thinks of Isaiah's two-bedroom suburban bungalow. How she could easily move in. It's more than big enough for two, she thinks. Maybe when she calls him back, she would propose an idea to him. She would stay over his house on Christmas Eve. She would wake up with him on Christmas morning. They would travel to his daughter's home together in his new car. His daughter would see Olive as more than just her father's friend. Maybe her father would too.

She calls him and gets his voicemail.

"Instead of picking me up on Christmas, how about the day before? I could cook some dinner, maybe stay over. Would save you a trip on Christmas day. Let me know." She shuts her phone, the interview and Wallace's question forgotten.

It's the day before Christmas Eve, several days since her interview with Verita Nolan. From articles she read about the job-hunting process, Olive knows that it may take longer than several days to receive word about her application status. She also knows from Stella that some places do not get back to applicants at all. Olive also remembers Verita Nolan's voicemail message about the interview, indicating they wanted to hire applicants before the holidays.

Olive recalls her interview, how Verita Nolan wanted Olive to consider one of their housekeeper openings, how Olive was adamant about expressing her sole interest in their administrative assistant position. She wonders if that was a mistake.

She calls Stainless-N-Spotless. When someone answers, she asks for Verita Nolan. She's transferred to her office.

"Verita Nolan."

"Hello, Miss Nolan, this is Olive Armnion. I interviewed with you last week."

"Oh, yes. I imagine you're calling about the administrative assistant position."

"Yes."

"We made an offer to another applicant yesterday. We were going to notify all applicants after the holidays. Thank you for applying and coming in for the interview, though. It was great meeting you."

Olive is about to say thank you when she hears a click on the other end. She pauses before she looks over at her grandsons. Usually, she would offer something witty to say. A wise word. She looks at them and waits for them to say something to her instead.

"We don't want you there, we want you here," Noah would say if he were here, she imagines. Of course they wouldn't want her to work, Olive thinks. How could she be available to babysit them?

She stares at their smiles and nods, confirming to herself that not getting that job is a good thing. They stare back at her, unmoving, stationary.

Olive wakes and sits up to peek outside her living room window. Light bits of snow fall. Snow usually annoys her, as it only represents obstacles to her travel. She doesn't mind it today. She knows Isaiah will be on his way to pick her up.

Ever since she last spoke to Verita Nolan, Olive has thought of spending more time with Isaiah in his car, in his gym, in his house. Olive had been successful with ignoring the rejection she received from Verita Nolan, pretending that she still had a chance, that all she had to do was wait for her cell phone to buzz. She wants her phone to do that now, to see Isaiah's name. She stares at her phone and wills it to buzz.

It does. She doesn't recognize the number. She answers it.

"Hello?"

"Olive! Thank God you picked up. I need you."

Olive recognizes the voice.

"How did you get my phone number?"

"The agency gave it to me. I have an emergency."

"Are you all right, Gertrude?"

"They're coming, Olive. My kids and their families. They were going to spend Christmas with their father's side of the family this year, but his wife got sick and had to check in at some hospital. It's like my gift came early!"

"And you're calling me today because …"

"I haven't cooked, cleaned, nothing. I want to make this big meal, but I can't do that and decorate the house at the same time. I need your help."

"Can't your kids help you?"

"I want everything ready before they get here. They'll arrive tomorrow morning. Can you come over?"

"I have plans. Sorry."

"I'll pay you double."

"No."

"Five hundred dollars. Just for your help a few hours today and tomorrow morning."

Olive hunches her shoulders. She looks at the white envelopes on her kitchenette's counter. She thinks of a counter of her own.

"Eight hundred," she says.

She hears Gertrude's surprise on the other end. "I think five hundred is much more than generous."

"So is working for you on Christmas Eve and Christmas Day on a few hours' notice."

"Fine, eight hundred. Can you get here soon?"

"In three hours."

"No sooner?"

"I have to shower. Pack my things. I also have to take two buses from where I live to your house. I'm sure you can understand. Have you ever had to deal with not having money?"

"I shared with you that I married rich. That I grew up having no money."

"So you just need a reminder of what it's like."

"Are you feeling all right, Olive?"

Olive sighs and wants to answer *no*. She wants to answer with a tone that would pinch Gertrude's ear.

"I'm fine," Olive says.

After moments of silence, Gertrude says, "I'm just excited. You know what that's like, right? When your adult children remember you exist? It's exhilarating." Gertrude laughs, the same kind of laughter she offers when they drink together at her house.

Olive doesn't reply. She knows the joy Gertrude is feeling. She doesn't know it well enough or often enough. She still knows it and chooses not to offer Gertrude her solidarity. Olive chooses instead to wait for her to say something else.

"Take your time," Gertrude eventually says. "See you soon."

Olive hangs up and snickers. She calls Isaiah. His voicemail answers. "It's me. Something came up. My customer needs me to help her prepare for her family's visit tomorrow. I can still go with you to your daughter's place, but I can't stay at your house tonight. Maybe you can pick me up tomorrow. She doesn't live far from you. She's on 9446 Everreed Court. I want us to go to your daughter's home together ..." Olive stops. She hangs up.

"Screw me," she says.

On Christmas Eve, Olive makes several mira-
cles. One looks and smells like a turkey, roasted to
perfection. Another comes in the form of a Christmas
tree, all decorated with shiny silver ornaments. The big-
gest one is Gertrude's house, the entire interior. All five
bedrooms with laundered linen, the kitchen cleaned
of all proof of Olive's cooking, the bathrooms shining
brighter than Gertrude's eyes.

Olive wants to enjoy Gertrude's excitement. She
understands what this Christmas will mean to her. She
knows how she would react if Geoffrey called to tell
her that he was coming to visit, taking a flight over
with Noah and Lionel.

Gertrude asks throughout the afternoon for them
to take breaks, offering her glasses of brandy. Olive
wants to say yes. Her knee joints and ankle are acting
up again, and she left her medication at home. But
she can't share Gertrude's enthusiasm with her over
brandy, not even a glass of merlot. On this Christmas
Eve and every other day, that's all they would ever share,
all Olive would have access to—glasses of temporary
consolation.

"No, need to keep working," she answers after each
request.

After the day becomes night, Gertrude offers Olive
one of her guest rooms. Lying on top of the bed she
made earlier that day, she sees that Isaiah left her a
voicemail on her cell phone. She listens to it, hoping
he has agreed to pick her up from Gertrude's house to-

morrow. He hasn't. He gives her his daughter's address and tells her he plans to arrive there in the morning.

She sighs, then calls Geoffrey. She hopes he has Noah and Lionel with him. He doesn't. He is instead hanging out with his new girlfriend, with whom he will spend Christmas Day. She asks him to tell Noah and Lionel a belated Merry Christmas for her when he picks them up the day after Christmas from their mother's house. Geoffrey doesn't ask Olive what her plans are. Instead, he wishes her a Merry Christmas and tells her that his gift to her is in the mail. Olive thanks him and hangs up.

On Christmas morning, she helps Gertrude wrap up gifts. She remembers her past Christmases when Geoffrey still lived with her, when he was a boy, the shuttling between her friends' and extended family members' houses. Olive never minded spending holidays at other homes mainly because her Christmas mornings belonged to Geoffrey. The two of them would open up each other's gifts by a small, undecorated Christmas tree in their living room. Back when Olive lived in a spacious two-bedroom apartment. Before her son shipped himself off to college and met his ex-girlfriend. The ex-girlfriend Olive didn't care for but thought she didn't need to. She was just someone temporary.

Until she became the mother to her grandsons.

Geoffrey had poorly treated the mother of her grandsons during their relationship. The mother of her grandsons decided that Geoffrey no longer needed to be her partner, thereby slashing his time as a father to Olive's grandsons to a quarter. Thereby reducing Olive's phone time with them to an eighth, feeling like a sixteenth. Feeling like nil.

Olive didn't send gifts for them to Geoffrey this year. She couldn't afford what Noah wanted, some mini electronic kid-sized sports car, and as for Lionel, she didn't want to send any forgettable presents to him or his brother. They had enough shirts and socks.

Olive asked Geoffrey during one of their phone conversations what he wanted this year. He said for his mother to be well and happy. No gift for him this year, she couldn't afford that either.

At this moment, what she can most afford is her time. She uses it proficiently to wrap the last set of gifts for Gertrude's children and grandchildren, humming solemn holiday tunes. After the last gift is wrapped, Olive sees that she's finished.

Gertrude doesn't ask Olive to leave. When Olive gathers her things, Gertrude offers her a glass of her finest merlot. Olive declines. Gertrude wants her to meet her family when they arrive. She says no, thank you. She should get going. She asks for her payment. Gertrude sighs, leaving the living room. She returns with a check. Olive takes it and says thank you.

Olive turns around to leave her house. She opens the

door and sees white. She wouldn't mind this if Isaiah's new black car were resting on Gertrude's long, winding driveway, adding a dark, shiny contrast to the snow, as if it were a sleek sleigh, waiting to carry her away.

She treads slowly down the walkway and makes her way to the bus stop.

Olive receives what she believes is the tightest hug she has ever had. She's cold and grumpy from her commute. She would have loved to arrive in a pretty holiday outfit. She's wearing jeans, a green sweater, and sneakers, with a gray coat. The makeup she applied in the morning has lost its luster. Her powder foundation barely withstood the snow that fell on her face.

Despite this, the long hug from Isaiah's daughter warms her into a better mood. "I'm Cammie. I'm glad you made it," she says, releasing her.

"Thanks for having me."

"Thank you for coming over. It's great to meet you," Cammie says. Olive steps farther inside her apartment and sees Isaiah sitting on the floor with Cammie's daughter, Georgia.

Isaiah doesn't look handsome today. His hair shines, and his face is freshly shaven. He's wearing a crisp, collared red shirt and thin black tie, with tailored black pants and shiny black leather shoes. He is an ad selling old-school cool. And yet, to Olive, he is not handsome today.

"Hello," Isaiah says. "Georgia, that's Olive. Can you say 'Merry Christmas'?"

Georgia, dressed in a pink dress and white stockings, waves her hand. Cammie leans toward Olive as if she will tell her a secret.

"She's quiet, but if you offer her candy, she'll become your best friend. Not even Daddy knows that."

"Good to know," Olive says.

Olive hums an upbeat holiday tune as she washes dishes. When Cammie apologized earlier about not preparing any food, Olive stepped up and stepped in. She offered to make them dinner, and when Cammie warmly reminded her that she was a guest, Olive pushed it further.

"Enjoy your time with them," she told her. "I have this."

Cammie relented, giving Olive her first Christmas gift of cooking for a family she now pretends is her own. Olive watches the three of them from Cammie's kitchen, thinking about the meal they finished eating ten minutes earlier.

Dinner was delicious, according to Cammie. "You should teach me how to cook!" she exclaimed to Olive after tasting her pork roast. Olive's second received Christmas gift.

Olive had waited for Isaiah's present. Which would have been for him to be present. To talk to her. To explain to her why he couldn't pick her up. His daughter redeems him with her enthusiasm.

Olive overhears her telling Isaiah that he should keep his girlfriend around. *Girlfriend.* The title rings like an ornament bell, light but pretty. Olive's third gift.

She can't wait until they leave Cammie's home before she asks him a question that has been tickling her nose like random lint since she left Gertrude's house.

"Cammie?" she calls out. "Would you mind if I borrowed your father for a minute?"

"Not at all," Cammie calls back. "Go to her, Daddy," Olive hears her gently coaxing Isaiah before he walks to the kitchen.

"My daughter really likes you," he says, standing next to her.

"Do you?" Olive asks.

"What do you mean?"

Olive dries a dish and sets it down on a wire rack by the sink. She picks up another dirty dish and stares at the tiny clumps of unfinished meat clinging to it.

"Did you get me something for Christmas?"

"You're not one to ask for gifts, Olive. That's what I like about you, you don't go hunting."

For the past several years, she has been hunting. Ever since she had to move out of her two-bedroom apartment because she no longer could afford the once-affordable rent. Ever since her doctor visits increased to where she couldn't keep track of her many ailments and bodily deficiencies. Ever since her life's work—working for other lives—had somehow sapped her own life through achy joints, weakened legs, and the absence of retirement funds.

"You do like me, then," Olive says. "What else do you like about me?"

"You're not on your phone all the time, typing away at nothing. You know Sam Cooke's music. You're easy to be with. There's no drama with you."

Unlike your twentysomethings, Olive thinks.

"You forgot beautiful and hot," she says. "Your other reasons why you call me. Because I'm beautiful and hot."

Isaiah says nothing.

"Screw you," Olive says.

"That too," Isaiah whispers. "I like it when you do."

"I meant that in a go-to-hell way."

Isaiah blinks his eyes as if he has just been woken up by an alarm. "Are you getting serious on me? I thought you were having a good time. I brought you here today because Cammie wanted to meet you."

"You didn't bring me," Olive snaps. "I took a bus."

"I'll drive you home, if that's what this is about," Isaiah says, lowering his voice. "You never came across as particular. I thought you were easygoing. Flexible."

Flexible. She is about to sputter the more vulgar version of screw you.

"I know why you like me," Isaiah continues. "It's not because of our meaningful conversations and deeply spiritual connection—we don't have those. That's okay with me. I thought that was fine with you."

Before Olive can disagree with him verbally and agree with him internally, her cell phone buzzes. She grabs it and flips it open.

"Hello?"

"Olive Armnion?"

"Yes," she confirms. She listens carefully as she watches Isaiah walking away to return to Cammie and Georgia in the living room. She learns that Wallace had a heart attack the previous evening while shopping. He's in the hospital. Olive's listed as his next of kin, the caller indicates. Olive is grateful that she's washing the last dish as she almost breaks it.

She shuts her cell phone and dries the last dish. She sets it with the rest of the clean dishes on the counter and moves to the living room. Both Isaiah and Cammie, sitting with Georgia on the sofa, look up at her.

"You look like you just got sad news," Isaiah says.

"You look like you care," Olive almost replies. He does look concerned. She has never seen that expression before on his face. If only he looked at her like that more often. Olive almost doesn't reply at all, just so she can hold that look with her eyes, her hands, all of her body.

"My friend had a heart attack and is in the hospital right now," she says. "I have to get there."

She notices from the corner of her eye how Cammie tightens her hold on her daughter. Olive recognizes this reaction to sad news—holding onto a loved one, like holding onto a banister on a staircase to keep balance, to keep standing, to not fall.

She holds her look on Isaiah, hoping he will stand up and walk over to her. She hopes—as if it would be her own holiday miracle—that he will say, "Let's go."

Olive's eyes widen as she sees him standing up and grabbing his jacket. Instead of placing it around his shoulders, he reaches into an inside pocket and takes out his cell phone.

"Your friend needs you right away," he says. "I'll call you a cab."

Olive feels the need to cry. She feels shame because it has nothing to do with her stricken friend.

Few things magnify someone's standing in another person's life more than a hospital stay. Who would call? Who would drop everything to show up?

Olive knew this well after her ankle operation. Two people visited. Geoffrey flew out, as it was his duty as Olive's only child to check up on her in person. Wallace was her other visitor. Seeing him outside of his apartment and their building was strange.

In the four years she has known Wallace, he has made it a point to never leave his apartment unless he's forced. Before he met Olive, his groceries were delivered to him and his television had the most updated cable with order-ready movies aplenty. Not that he watches much television. His primary entertainment is reading. Wallace reads and rereads at least three books a week. As a former school principal by route of being an English teacher, he appreciates literature the way Olive appreciates red wine.

She also knows that Wallace rarely leaves his apartment for visits because he doesn't have family and friends who would in turn leave their homes to visit him.

After Olive's operation, Wallace left his home. He showed up to see her dressed in a blue collared shirt, green sweater, and brown pleated pants, his creased chocolate skin shining on his face. He brought his mahogany cane, even though Olive could tell he tried not to use it, taking three steps at a time before conceding to lean on it for support. In his other hand were two books.

It was the most handsome he had ever looked to Olive; she even smelled cologne lingering in the air after he sat down on a chair next to her hospital bed. She looked at him, and the effort of his trip and neatness of his dress made him desirable.

"You look like shit," Wallace said.

Her desire left. No hint of joking. An observation. It reminded Olive that her friend would never tell her a lie, even if she needed to hear one.

"What brings you here?"

Wallace shrugged. "Figured no one else would come to see you."

"You're wrong. My son was here."

"Was? He left already?"

"His flight leaves tonight."

"I saw a man downstairs with a mustache and beard wearing a red sweater. Was that him?"

"Yes."

"He made no arrangements for you?"

"He doesn't make much money and lives on the other side of the country. What can he do for me?"

"What he should," he said, standing up from the chair. He plopped the books on her lap. "You're going to be bored. Read these to pass the time."

"Where are you going?"

"Out," Wallace replied.

"Will you be back?"

"I have no choice."

Sitting in the backseat of the cab Isaiah called for her, Olive now understands what he meant. Like Wallace, Olive had no choice but to leave Cammie's apartment after the phone call. It was the same pull that would have come from a call about her son, automatic, frantic, dutiful.

Wallace is like the immediate family she was born into, someone she's stuck with, gladly or not, someone she can't divorce, someone who will always be there, waiting for her to visit, waiting for her to stop by.

OLIVE ARRIVES AT THE EMERGENCY ROOM AND IS DI-rected to another ward. Seeing an administrative nurse, she asks for Wallace. She directs her to a room down the hall. Olive reaches it and peeks inside. She sees Wallace wearing a white hospital gown lying on a half-folded-up bed. When she enters his room, she finds herself ready to snap at him. Before she does, she notices a small blue square box resting on a table by his bed.

"What were you doing at the mall, Wallace?"

He opens his eyes. "It took you a while. Were you at your boyfriend's?"

"He's not my boyfriend."

"Did he bring you here?"

"I took a cab."

"He couldn't drive you?"

"What were you doing at the mall?"

Wallace motions toward the blue box with his head. "That's for you."

Olive glances at it but doesn't reach for it. "I was told over the phone that you had collapsed outside of a store."

"One that sells jewelry," Wallace confirms. "If I was at home, you'd have received a different call, probably weeks later. One saying I was dead. Making that trip saved my life. I should thank you."

The bulk of his words lands on her shoulders. She knows she wouldn't have received a call. She would have instead found him days later on the floor in his apartment. Maybe slumped over his recliner.

"My lifesaver there is yours to keep, to sell, to do whatever you like with."

"Why did you buy this? We don't need a ring to get married."

"You may need one to agree to it."

"I'm not some young thing who gets blinded by bling."

"Bling? What the hell is a bling?"

"I don't love you."

"You don't want me," Wallace corrects. "But you do care for me. Not like you do that boyfriend of yours. But that's fine."

The word 'boyfriend' stings Olive. "If you want me around all the time," she says, sighing, "I can just move in with you."

"When I die, you'd get everything. I don't want Harold getting my shit. He doesn't deserve shit. He is shit."

Olive thinks his brother should have been called instead of her. "He's your next of kin."

"I'm not the next of his," Wallace says. Olive knows he refers to Harold's wife and six children. "I called him, you know, after the hospital called you. I told my bitch of a brother that I was here, and he told me to get well soon. After fifteen years, he says, 'Get well soon.'"

His eyes well. Olive can't take looking at them. It's as if she's looking at her own. She shifts her gaze to the blue box.

"I'm going to tell you no, Wallace. You should know that."

"I need to rest, Olive. Please take the ring with you.

I don't want anybody stealing it while I'm sleeping. I'm mighty shocked that nobody has taken it from me yet."

Enough of the bullshit, Olive silently snaps, looking at Wallace again, ignoring their surroundings, suppressing her pity.

"Why do you want to marry me?"

Olive knows what his answer will be, waiting for him to spill it. "You'll be legally bound to me," he will say. "You'll have access to my pension, perhaps life insurance and all of my assets, and in return you'll wash my clothes, cook my meals, pick up my medication, listen to my stories, touch me, make love to me, and maybe even love me, not because you want to, but because you'll be my wife and you'll have to, by law of country and God," he will list out.

He will cap it off with, "And I don't want to die alone."

As soon as he says all that, Olive will reply with a resounding no. She waits.

"You're something I thought I would never have again," Wallace says.

"What would that be? A pretty woman in your home, cleaning and cooking?"

"A good friend," he answers. "A pretty good friend. I can be one to you."

Olive smiles a little, surprising herself. Wallace's eyes no longer brim with liquid. She's grateful.

"You're not pretty," she says.

"Not like that boyfriend of yours, no. But I'd take care of you."

Olive can no longer ignore their surroundings. Beeping noises. The IV in his arm. His bed with gray rails on both sides, looking like a sterile crate.

After a few moments, she says, "You're already a good friend to me. That's why I came."

Wallace turns his head toward the room's only window. "Thanks for stopping by, Olive."

"You want me to come by tomorrow?"

"Do whatever you like. Just take the ring with you, please," Wallace replies, shutting his eyes. "If I'm not here tomorrow, you know where I live."

Olive takes the small blue box and places it in her bag. She walks out of the room into the bright hallway.

OLIVE TAKES OUT HER COPY OF WALLACE'S KEYS. It has been two weeks since she last used them, when she broke down in his living room, the day he proposed. She opens his door and smells a light funk of cigarettes. He has taken up smoking again, she deduces.

She remembers when he explained to her years ago why he moved out of his three-bedroom, two-story house to this apartment. He said that his home was getting wider as he was getting thinner. He didn't want to pay property taxes and maintenance costs for a space he no longer felt big in. He sold his house at a huge profit and would use that money, along with his pension and other assets, to maintain himself affordably in this building in one of its few unsubsidized units. Olive recalls how she thought he was silly to sell away what she would have given almost anything to own.

She no longer thinks that. Setting her bag on his recliner, she looks around the space, trying to determine what she should do first. His laundry? His dishes?

She settles on his floor. She walks over to the closet in his hallway and takes out his vacuum. With its help, she sucks dirt from his carpet in broad strokes with her right arm, feeling a dull ache in her shoulder. She ignores it and washes dishes in his kitchen.

Olive takes her bag and walks over to his bedroom. She lies down on his bed and smells cigarettes again. She decides that she'll do his laundry in the morning. She will make his bedroom and the rest of his apartment fresh.

Fresh. That's why she loves to clean, wash, wipe away. She makes things new again.

New. She grabs the blue velvet box from her bag. She opens it and finds light. A silver ring closed by one square-shaped stone of sparkles. This is the first diamond ring that she has ever been given. Her ex-husband, Geoffrey's father, proposed only with a shrug.

If Isaiah had presented her with this ring, she would have cried. Out of joy and disbelief. Olive is shedding tears now. Out of gratitude and resignation. She decides to put her career-changing job search on hold.

The stack of white envelopes will no longer be her burden alone.

She places the box next to her on Wallace's bed and grabs her bag. She takes out her cell phone. She waits for her tears to stop dropping. Once they do, she calls Isaiah. It goes to his voicemail.

"Thank you for calling me a cab," she begins. "My friend's heart attack was mild. It looks like he'll be fine. Listen, I don't think we'll be seeing each other again. Thank your daughter for me, she's a good girl. Take good care of yourself…wait, you already do that." She shuts her cell phone and laughs. Her laughs become sobs.

Wiping tears and the remaining makeup off her cheeks with the back of her right hand, Olive shakes her head. She knows what will happen when she visits Wallace tomorrow, bringing him two books from his apartment.

"Okay," she will whisper in his ear, placing his books by his lap on the hospital bed, where he will see, on her left ring finger, a square of light.

Lost, Never Had

MY MOTHER LOST HER MAN, LOST HER COOL, LOST HER KEYS MORE TIMES THAN SHE COULD COUNT BUT NEVER LOST HER CON-viction. At least that's what she wrote in her journal. I found it in the back corner of her closet, years after she lost it, two days after she died.

Inside her journal rested a gold necklace with a cross. The first page said, "God is great." The second page had scripture passages. The tenth page said, "I thank God for my husband." The thirtieth page said, "I thank God for my daughter." The forty-seventh page said, "I thank God for my husband leaving me." The fifty-third page said, "Please Father, keep him away from me. Keep him away from Ifama."

Ifama is my name. My name means all is well in Igbo. That's how my mother felt after I was born. That I didn't have to read in her journal—that's what she told me repeatedly before she died. All was well when God brought you to me and all is well now, she told me, her eyes convincing me each time. All is well, my dear, all is well.

All wasn't well after I was born. My father turned into someone new, someone unhappy. As the doctor cut my umbilical cord, I became free while my father became the opposite—forever tethered to my mother by my existence.

My mother told me he lost his faith after what many would call a miracle showed up. Instead of saying, "Praise God," he said, "No, God, no."

My mother, drugged from her exhaustion, could still hear his words, "No, God, no." She hoped he was thinking of something else, maybe he forgot to pay a bill.

I believe he lost his mind. And his patience. Both my parents were twenty years old when I was born. Both were immigrants, as their parents moved from Nigeria to the U.S. with plans of sending their children to American universities. They both met in college at a Christian club meeting, both marveling to learn that not only were they from the same country and same tribe but their families were also from the same village. Cups of faith, sprinkles of fate. Then my mother learned she was late.

My father married my mother after she told him she was pregnant. Both sets of their parents demanded the marriage. I imagined my mother's unearned shame turned into unearthed joy when I arrived, while my father's anxiety birthed aggravation. My newborn cries made it official—his promising youth was over.

So was any chance for him to know if he could have loved my mother for who she was, not for whom she carried. They moved in together into a two-bedroom apartment close to their campus. Their parents helped them, purchasing items they could afford, my crib, diapers, bottles. It was their parents' mission for their children to finish college and go to medical school, regardless of my existence.

My mother believed her future wasn't spoiled. My father might have believed differently about his own. Even while he continued going to church after my birth, he stopped praying, stopped praising, stopped paying tithes, her journal said. That's when she believed he lost his faith.

That's the question I will ask my father when I see him later this afternoon, seeing him for the first time after twenty years of absence and silence. I won't ask him what he has been up to or if he ever thought about me.

I will ask him if he lost his faith after he first found my voice.

My father found me on the Internet. I imagine he typed my name into a search engine and reviewed the results until he saw something that looked enough like me. He found my website. I write a blog about movies, television shows, cartoons—all kinds of stories I watch on a screen. Only a handful of people have read my blog, and people who write comments on it have been fewer.

I have a contact page with my e-mail address. I put it there hoping someone would find it, maybe a stranger in Los Angeles who would also happen to be an executive at some studio and she would e-mail me directly and write: "Ifama, you have an *eye* for film and television, and I want to fly you out here, and together, we will make art *and* make bank." I checked my inbox daily waiting for that e-mail.

Two weeks ago, I received a potentially life-changing e-mail from a stranger but not an executive in Los Angeles. From a man who wrote that he was my father. A man whose name I instinctively knew and recognized.

He could have reached out to my uncle Ekwueme, my mother's brother, but perhaps he was afraid. According to my uncle's wife, my aunt Chiamaka, Uncle Ekwueme beat him bloody after my father did the same to my mother. Aunt Chiamaka often spoke about this with pride, saying she knew she would marry Ekwueme when she witnessed him pummel my father.

My father was twenty-two and Uncle Ekwueme was a year older. Ekwueme's parents, my grandparents, chastised him when they heard of the developments, saying he shouldn't do anything to risk his station in the States. My grandparents moved back to Nigeria to retire after their youngest child, my mother, started college here in the U.S.

My grandparents' friendship with my father's parents—the other set of grandparents whom I have never met—ended swiftly after they learned their son's brother-in-law thrashed him. My grandparents defended their son Ekwueme even though they regretted his actions privately within their side of the family. The other set of grandparents insisted that whatever happened between a man and his wife was the man's business and his business alone. Uncle Ekwueme shared a different opinion, punching his perspective onto my father's face with his fist.

"I will do it again," Uncle Ekwueme told me after I told him a week ago that I was going to meet my father for lunch at a restaurant out-of-state, a fancy one on the outskirts of Philadelphia.

I was visiting their apartment in Newark for an afternoon, busying myself in their kitchen preparing ogbono soup. Both Uncle Ekwueme and Aunt Chiamaka often marvel at how well I prepare traditional dishes, having traveled to Nigeria only twice. I have never told them that I mastered the delicious dishes to keep myself useful to them. If I ever tell them that, they will reprimand me, reminding me that I am their daughter and have always been since my mother died.

I am not their daughter. They care for me like one of their own, but that line, many times invisible, shows its shadow during any conversation in which they make family decisions focusing solely on their sons.

That afternoon was one of those times, and this time I was the one making a family decision to meet with my father, this decision excluding my uncle. I could tell he was aggravated because he didn't forbid me to meet the man whom he wanted to punch again. My father's parental line—rarely acknowledged—would never be erased, would never become invisible.

"If he hurts you like he did to my sister, he will have to pray to God to stop me."

"I don't think it's going to be like that," I said, turning down the heat on the stove. "He's not going to hurt me."

Uncle Ekwueme looked angry, annoyed, *and* apprehensive. I didn't know a look like that was possible.

"You do not know him. If you do not know him, how do you know what he will or will not do?"

Uncle Ekwueme had a point. I didn't know my father, and I don't know him still. I know his name, and from the only picture I have of him, I know his face. I didn't even search his name online.

As I prepped the ingredients an hour before my uncle's declaration, Aunt Chiamaka advised him that meeting my father would be the best thing for me. I wasn't technically eavesdropping because this counsel took place in their living room, which is open to their kitchen. I tried to hum to myself to provide a wall between their voices and my ears, but my song wasn't loud enough.

Aunt Chiamaka told him I needed to meet my father. She said their stories about him meant very little because I needed to see it for myself. She reminded her husband that I was no longer a kid, I was all of twenty-two, and as an adult, I needed to make my own decisions about the people I would allow in my life.

"She needs clarification on who the man is," my uncle countered.

"More than that, she needs closure," my aunt rebutted. "We are unable to provide that."

"He will hurt her."

"Ifama is not your sister."

"What do you mean?"

"Your sister saw signs of who the man was very early, did she not? She stayed with him until he left and would have stayed with him even longer if he had not left. Ifama will not wait that long. God will not let her stay around."

"He is an idiot," he sputtered.

"The idiot is her father. He will always be. That is why she needs to meet him," my aunt said, speaking irrefutable data.

"I will go with her."

"You will not. We are older now. That wretched man is too, and so is Ifama—she is an adult woman now. She needs to handle her own life, and she will, quite effectively. Am I correct, Ifama?"

I increased the volume of my humming. Aunt Chiamaka and I are not related by blood, yet we are very close. I think that is partly due to her not having daughters of her own.

"Am I correct?" she asked out loud again.

"Yes, Aunty, you are right. As always."

"Yes! As always. Our niece is smart."

I wanted to agree with her. Worried about meeting this stranger who hurt my mother, I didn't.

I'M SITTING HERE IN A RESTAURANT OUTSIDE OF PHIL-adelphia, one that I recently saw on a television program featuring five-star dining establishments. I peruse the menu. The entrees are priced in the forties and fifties. I'm wondering if my father will pay for this or if I'm expected to pay for myself.

I arrived here thirty minutes ago, driving from Newark. I don't live with Uncle Ekwueme and Aunt Chiamaka anymore, though I still live in their neighborhood, just a few streets away in a small studio apartment.

This restaurant is larger than my studio, but this table feels tiny. I look around, and there are only a few diners, and now I want there to be more people. I want this place to be packed. I want noise and chatter and busyness. There is no music playing, and my phone is almost out of battery.

I don't want to go out to the parking lot to retrieve my charger because it's almost 4:00 p.m., and my father will be here soon—if he is a punctual person. I don't want to risk seeing him getting out of his own car in the parking lot. I want to be sitting at this table when he gets here. I want him to see me waiting. I want him to feel ashamed for making me wait in this restaurant I can't afford to dine in.

Folding my hands on the table, I try to look like a boss, like the CEO of our bankrupt corporation, our depleted family. I should have worn a business suit. Or maybe my black graduation gown that would make me look like a judge without the cap. My phone could be my gavel. Instead of banging it on the table, I would swipe to a picture of my beautiful mother, hold it up to my father's face, and then ask: *Regrets?*

I'm regretting my outfit. I'm wearing black jeans, blue flats, and a mahogany turtleneck. My hair is a small afro. I look nice, but what I should look like is *mean*. A scowl here, a snicker there. I look down at my hands, as they are now fidgeting with my phone.

I exhale, realizing I have been holding my breath for a minute. I look down on my lap, my mother's brown journal resting on it. I brought it just in case I'm persuaded to read it out loud as a response to any questions my father might ask me. I take my mother's journal and rest it on the table next to my phone, which is now at three percent.

The time says 4:00 p.m. I look at the entrance and keep my eyes there. If he doesn't walk in before it turns to 4:01 p.m., the first full sentence he'll hear from his daughter will be, "You're tardy."

He already is. Years late.

I see the door open. My phone still says 4:00 p.m.

MY MOTHER GAVE BIRTH TO ME EARLY, WHEN SHE was seven months pregnant, and left me early, dying when I was seventeen and she was thirty-seven, but she was late for almost everything else in between. She was late arriving to work, late getting to family functions, sometimes she made me late for school, but one place she never arrived late was church.

For five years, she attended a church that held its services in a small conference room at a hotel in a town on the outskirts of Newark. I forget its name, but I'll never forget her fervor on Sunday mornings, wearing a dress with floral print and shoes with low heels and pointed tips and ensuring her hair was smoothed back, no strands out of place. Her nails were always shiny and red, and she smelled like a blend of fruits. She would read her Bible in her bedroom before entering our living room and announcing herself: "I am ready."

I was always ready before her, not because I was excited to attend church. I didn't want to let her down. I made sure I looked as polished as her. I knew that made her happy.

"I'm ready too," I'd say.

What I never felt ready for was arriving at the church, the way some of the ladies there would greet my mother and the way some of them would talk to me. Well-intended but condescending statements like, "You *must* read your Bible every day" (assuming I hadn't) and "You are losing weight, good for you!"

My mother loved that church of thirty people. She loved the singing, the praising, the worship, and her fellow members. The last Sunday we attended was a day of extra celebration. The pastor, a gregarious man, announced that the church was going to move out of the conference room in the hotel to a rundown and closed-down church in the same town. The new church was a building of stone with a tall steeple and magenta double doors. It came with its own wooden benches, a podium, and an organ. From tithes and collections, enough money was saved for a down payment on the property. My mother donated half of her savings, one thousand dollars. She said it was her greatest tithe.

My mother's smile lit up the conference room all throughout service. Her Hallelujahs and Amens were soft, but her smile was loud. Moving out of the hotel and into an established church space must have meant more to her than a shorter commute on Sunday mornings. Moving forward was something she couldn't do often after she divorced my father. She never went on to medical school. She never remarried, never dated. We didn't even leave the two-bedroom apartment she and my father first moved into before I was born.

After service, the pastor spoke to some of the members until his eyes met my mother's face. He motioned for her to meet him in the hallway leading to the hotel's lobby. She followed him out there, and I thought nothing of it until twenty minutes later when she returned with reddened eyes. She walked over to me and grabbed my hand.

"We're leaving," she said.

I followed her out of the conference room and out of the hotel into a sun-filled parking lot where we usually waited for the church's van to take us home. Instead, we walked through the lot, past parked cars and painted lines to the bus stop on the corner.

I studied her face once we got there. Dried tears tinged the makeup on her cheeks. She looked up to the sky.

"When a man tries to touch you in a way you don't want," she said, her head still facing upward, "you kick him between his legs. No hesitation."

"Okay," I said.

I never viewed the pastor as my shepherd. I just sat and listened to his sermons. I didn't see him as my direct phone line to God.

I think my mother did. Maybe she gleaned her faith from people, specifically the pastor. Maybe before that church, she drew faith from my father.

Was their first meeting at their college's Christian club like that? Did he preach to her privately, purposefully? Was she drawn to his resolute knowledge of the Bible shared through his charming eyes and baritone voice?

Did she see him as a sign from God? Maybe her gift from God?

I still wonder about that. I never wondered about my mother's tears—they were absolute, like her conviction. When we returned home that Sunday, my ears snatched the sound of her sobs and dispatched her distress to my own eyes.

Two days after she died, when I found her journal, I

flipped through pages to an entry that read, "Lord, why lead me to those who worship you yet try to spoil me?"

The next page read, "I will never stop believing in You. You are not the pastor, You are not the people, You are You. I find You everywhere and anywhere. Not in just one place, not in just one church and not in one person. You are my guide. Amen."

MY PHONE STILL SAYS 4:00 P.M. WHEN THE RESTAU-rant's door opens and a tall man walks in. I recognize his face, yet it is slightly different from the old photo—now rounder. There are a few creases around his eyes. His face is mostly the same. His face is mostly my face.

He wears a black trench coat, a purple tie, and a collared white shirt with black slacks. He's wearing thin-rimmed eyeglasses. He looks around and sees me. He smiles wide, his face becoming joyful, like he's just learned he has won the lottery. Like his life is now set.

He walks toward my table and stands in front of me.

"Ifama! Look at you! You're not going to give your father a hug?"

"No," I answer. I extend my hand to point to the other chair. His smile recedes a tad. He takes off his coat and folds it over the other chair. He sits.

"I wanted to meet with you for a long time," he says. "I'm glad you answered my e-mail. Please, ask the waiter for menus so we can order."

"You ask the waiter," I say, leaning against my chair,

crossing my arms. "I'm the one who drove for two hours to be here."

His smile is now gone altogether. He raises his hand to motion over a waiter.

"I asked you to travel here because I'd like to bring you to my house so you can meet my wife. She is very excited to meet you."

Wife. Before I say anything, the waiter arrives and takes our orders. I get an appetizer, a small plate of calamari. He orders a full entrée, lobster with a mixed-greens salad. He waves the waiter away. He doesn't say thank you.

"You graduated from college, right?" he asks me.

"Yes. Almost a year ago."

"Good, good. What did you major in?"

"I double majored in psychology and chemistry."

"Pre-med?"

"Yes."

"Applying to medical schools?"

"No. I changed my mind."

"What are you doing now?"

"I'm working toward a career in pharmaceuticals," I reply. The last film I wrote about on my blog was about two people who met and fell in love outside of a pharmacy. Close enough.

"Good for you. There is longevity in that field. I'm a pharmacist."

"You're not a doctor?"

"Yes. I have a doctorate in pharmaceutical sciences. I am not a medical doctor, if that is what you mean."

"Do you regret not going to medical school?"

"When you believe in God, you don't have regrets. Just mercies." He folds his hands on the table. "Do you believe in God, Ifama?"

"Why do you ask?"

"I need to make sure you are saved."

"Are you saved?" I ask him.

"Yes. I want to talk to you about your life," he says. "My pastor tells me that I need to make things right with you as I continue to make things right with God."

"How do you think you'll accomplish that?"

"By making sure you know God," he answers. "As your father, that's my duty."

I laugh.

"Don't ever, *ever* laugh at God," he warns.

"I'm not laughing at God," I say. "I'm laughing at you."

"This is not humorous."

I stop laughing and look straight at him.

"You are acting rude," he says.

"You know what's rude? Not saying 'thank you.'"

"Enough."

"Not used to people calling you out?"

"Enough!"

The anger on his face should scare me, but instead I find myself enraged mixed with a little bit of bitter. The waiter arrives with plates of lobster and calamari. The waiter looks tense, as if he heard my father's yell from the kitchen and preferred to stay there. I tell the waiter thank you. My father, again, does not.

My hands switch from resting on my mother's journal to holding it. "Did you lose your faith after I was born?"

He looks back at me.

"I'm curious," I say. "Once I got here, like got here on earth, did you lose your faith?"

He now looks calm. "No," he replies. "I lost my vision."

I say nothing.

"Before I met your mother, I could see ahead. I made a mistake, we made you, and it made things blurry. I could no longer see my future because I couldn't see past you and your mother. I wasn't ready. It was all too much."

I should thank him for his honesty. Instead, I clench my jaw and clutch my mother's journal tighter.

"When I met my wife two years ago, it was like being able to see again. She got me back into church, got me back on the right road, a bright road. God blessed me with her. We're expecting our first child in two months. A girl."

I should say congratulations.

"The pastor told me you were the key to my penance. It was my wife, however, who convinced me to search for you and e-mail you. My own parents and siblings never encouraged me to reach out to you, not once. They never told me to do the right thing. God-fearing, all of them, yet they never told me to fight for you. My wife was the only one who saw light in *me*. And only light can see light. That bright light of my wife told me you deserved your father. So, I'm here."

He smiles wide like he just ended a sermon with a promise of salvation. As if my mother's journal I'm holding is my Bible and this upscale restaurant is a trendy church. As if I'm not only his daughter but also one of his parishioners. I'm a prisoner.

I sit here immobilized, looking at his face. I feel like crying, but I'm not sure what for. I don't know whether to say Amen or good-bye.

He looks at our plates as if they are keys to brand-new convertibles. He looks at me and extends his arm across the table, holding his palm out.

"Let us pray," he says.

Let us pray. Those were my grandfather's last words before I left the village three hours north of Lagos where my mother spent most of her childhood. It was the day after my mother's burial. Uncle Ekwueme was there with his siblings, and Aunt Chiamaka stayed back in New Jersey with their boys, as they couldn't afford all the airfare. My other uncles, their spouses and kids, were there, along with a number of great-aunts and great-uncles with second and third cousins.

We all gathered into a huddle, holding hands, holding shoulders, praying for my mother and for our safe travels to our respective homes. With every passing day between when she died and her burial, the ache in my shoulders, chest, and neck subsided. I cried less. When Uncle Ekwueme and I flew to Nigeria and drove three hours to our family's village, my tears stopped altogether.

After my grandfather said, "Let us pray," Uncle Ekwueme led the prayer. He was my mother's closest brother. He prayed for her spirit and for healing. He prayed for everyone to travel safely. He ended the prayer with words of gratitude. I felt thankful to God that I had a family—that I had people surrounding me, people who held my hand and had my back.

When Uncle Ekwueme and I returned to New Jersey, that huddle didn't travel with me. I moved into their three-bedroom apartment, as they cleared one of their sons' rooms for me. I was going to leave for college the following year anyway, but I knew I was already alone.

I didn't fully understand this until Christmastime arrived. Uncle Ekwueme and his family left for Lagos to visit Aunt Chiamaka's parents and sisters, who were not my grandparents and aunts. They couldn't afford my airfare, and while I had a bit of savings, I had to leave that alone because I no longer had my mother to count on for money.

Aunt Chiamaka felt guilty about leaving without me, so I poured on my happiness, bragging about how I would have their whole apartment to myself. I taunted them about how I would throw a big holiday party in their absence.

That Christmas Day, the first one without my mother, I did throw a party. A party of one. I sat in their living room and watched reruns of *Living Single*, wishing I lived inside their flat-screen television in a beautiful Brooklyn brownstone with my best friends, all of us living together as one family unit. My mother's journal rested on the empty cushion next to me. I didn't read her words that day. I didn't feel her presence.

I thought about my father, wondering if he also was visiting Nigeria, visiting his family, wondering if he knew his ex-wife had died, if he was concerned about me. Maybe word got around to him, and maybe after learning about it, he shed tears. Maybe he knelt on a floor somewhere and prayed for me.

MY FATHER'S PALM IS STILL OPEN ON THE TABLE.

"Let us pray," he repeats, waiting for me to take his hand.

I fold my hands together on my mother's journal instead and close my eyes, even though I almost keep them open to see the expression on his face. He prays over the food, then he thanks God for our opportunity to dine together in this ritzy restaurant, prays for me to find and serve God, then he prays for me to act like a child of God, then he prays for me to read my Bible and for me to know the importance of a father in a child's life. He says Amen.

Opening my eyes, I see him gather his utensils to eat.

I close my eyes again, keeping my hands folded on my mother's journal. I clear my throat and I speak a prayer. I pray to God to rid me of my anger. My voice is crystal, both clear and defined, impossible to ignore. I continue to pray for my father and his new family. I pray for my father to not hurt his new wife like he hurt my mother. I pray for him to be a good father to his new daughter when she arrives, to lead her by his example and not his testimony. I pray he doesn't mistake pressuring for preaching, intimidation for inspiration. I pray for mercy for both of us. I pray for my father to never forget my mother's face if he forgets that he is not the center of the world.

I open my eyes and see my mother's journal. I look up and see my father standing by the restaurant's front door, holding his coat, looking at me, looking disappointed.

"Why did you treat my mother like that?" I loudly ask him.

He leaves. Tears streaming from my eyes, steam still rising from his plate of lobster, I raise my hand to ask for the check.

MY DRIVE BACK HOME IS LONG, AS TRAFFIC ON THE New Jersey Turnpike is heavy. My mother's journal sits on the passenger side close to me. My phone is on silent inside my bag in the backseat, just in case someone calls or texts me. I only want to talk to my mother.

I reach the apartment building where I live in a studio apartment on the first floor. I find a parking spot by the building and turn off my car's ignition. I grab my mother's journal and my bag and step out of my car. I walk to the entryway. Aunt Chiamaka stands by the locked glass door.

"Is your phone off again?" she asks me.

"I silenced it. It's probably out of battery by now anyway."

"Did you have a good meeting with your father?"

"Are you asking or Uncle Ekwueme?"

"Both of us. We are worried about you."

"No need," I say, opening the building's door with my keys. "You can come in, but my place is a hot mess."

"I need to return home," Aunt Chiamaka says. "Which is also your home."

I disagree but nod anyway, appreciating her words. "Thank you, Aunty. I'll see you next week."

She hugs me. Summoning all the strength left in my jaw and shoulders, I stop myself from sobbing.

"Did you receive the answers to your questions about him? You can always ask your uncle and me. We will tell you anything you need to know about that man. We are always here for you."

"Good night," I say. She lets me go, and I let myself into the building. I close its glass door, Aunt Chiamaka

still standing on the other side. I know without looking that she's watching me walk away, waiting until
I disappear into my home before she returns to hers.

My e-mail's log-in screen is bright. I type in my
password. It's almost 10 p.m. here in my studio. Curiosity keeps me awake, keeps my eyes blinking light and
dark, screen and blank. Curiosity compelled me to meet
with my father in person in the first place. Curiosity, I
realize, is not always helpful.

I type in my password and see one new e-mail. It's
the newest message in a continuing thread of e-mails
that started with the first one I realize now I should
have deleted. If only forgetting and deleting were the
same thing. I could just delete today like I will delete
this e-mail, knowing that I'll probably still remember
every single word my father typed.

> Ifama,
>
> Today did not go the way I prayed for. Life
> does not move backward. Neither do I. If you
> want to meet my wife and your new sister
> after she's born, please write back and indi-
> cate so. I will then e-mail you my address
> and you can come visit us.
>
> If not, we must then part ways. I pray God
> will bless you all your days and that He will

give you a good attitude and wisdom to do
the right thing.

I do not click delete. I click reply.

You owe me $49.50, including tip. I'll waive
what you owe me if you don't ever write to
me again.

I've been moving forward, just looking back-
ward once in a while. If I meet your new
family, I'll just be looking back, trying to find
things missing I never had to begin with. I
don't know if you get it, you might understand, you might not.

If you understand, then please know I forgive
you. If you don't, I still forgive you.

Have a wonderful life. Don't hit your new
wife.

I click send. I grab my mother's journal and turn to
the last page she wrote.

*I forgive all who have wronged me as I pray You forgive
me.*

I read her words aloud. I repeat them. I mean them.

I remove the gold cross necklace bookmarking my
mother's journal for years. I wrap it around my neck
and clasp it. I close her journal and place it by my laptop.

I finally shut down my computer and turn off my studio's lights. I kneel down by my sofa bed and say a prayer. I say Amen. I keep my eyes closed, waiting for my loneliness to leave me, waiting for my prayer to be answered, keeping my conviction that it will.

Speakers &
Headphones

I SEE SERINE.

But it's not her. It's Regina who's walking toward me, and her hair is different. Ever since we met during our freshman year at college, three-plus years ago, she has always kept her hair in box braids, like me. No more braids, her natural hair is now her extensions, her strands extending from her scalp to the world.

She smiles at me. "Juuuune!"

I wave my hand, but I don't rise from my chair. Outside a café on the Upper West Side, I'm sitting by a small, round table. On it, a bowl of bread waits, along with butter packets, menus, and two glasses of water I ordered for us. She reaches me, crouches down, and gives me a hug. I tap her back lightly. She releases me, grabs the other chair, and sits.

"What do you think?"

I scan her appearance. The navy blue shirtdress looks good on her, especially with her afro, but her outfit is not new, she wears it every other week. I'm guessing she wants to know what I think of her hairstyle. The one that Serine would have worn, I'm supposing, if I had truly seen her, if we still knew each other.

"Your hair looks beautiful."

"Thank you," she says. "But I was referring to my problem. Tell me what you think."

We're on spring break. We both happen to be home in New York this week. When we're not living together on campus, I live with my mother up in the Bronx, and Regina lives with her folks in Crown Heights. She called my cell phone this morning with good news, saying that we had to meet today in the middle—Manhattan—for an emergency talk.

She received acceptance letters from both law schools she applied to. Her first choice is a big name. The other, her safety school, which offered her a full-tuition scholarship, is one she doesn't care to attend.

Instead of responding, I sip my water.

"What should I take?" Regina presses. "Free ride or prestige?"

I still don't reply. I enjoy her company because she has a cheerful spirit that should annoy me but oddly doesn't. She likes mine because, according to her, my talk lacks bull. It doesn't. She thinks that I always tell it straight only because my talk lacks talk.

I won't ever tell her why I keep my words few. Telling her would make us close.

IN 1995, I USED TO TALK BULL EVERY DAY.

Almost every weekday morning during seventh and eighth grades, I walked toward White Plains Road and waited for Serine in an area where that road and

Boston Road met. Almost every morning, I would see her speed-walking toward me, wearing her headphones connected to her portable cassette player.

Her head and body bobbed as she walked. She had this bounce, as if music flowed through her veins, the notes coming through her headphones working as her heartbeats. She would sing along with the music or rap to it, sometimes she would hum.

Whereas I would talk. I would chat her ear off all the way to school. She would listen, only offering a word or two to keep me talking, singing or humming in between my spurts of words about minutiae.

After school, she would walk me home. My mother and I lived in the upper part of the Bronx, on a street right off Boston Road in a three-story apartment complex, each story its own apartment.

Inside of our two-bedroom apartment, our kitchenette opened up to our living room, lined with an old carpet where Serine and I would sit and watch cartoons. She would nod, sing, hum, but not talk. Talking was my gift, my hobby. It was gold to have someone hold on to my words.

We met at the start of seventh grade. I was new at my middle school, as my mother and I had just moved from Brooklyn up to the Bronx. I wasn't homesick, because I didn't have any friends back in Brooklyn. Every weekday, I went to school and returned home.

All the way up in the Boogie Down after my third day at my new school, two older boys followed me, calling me names as they walked a few feet behind me. Afraid to run, thinking it would've been an invitation for them to chase me, also guessing that I couldn't outrun them, I entered a bodega on the corner.

A few moments later, they walked in. One of them approached me and told me to follow them outside. Serine appeared from the other side of one of the mini-aisles, truly coming out of nowhere, wearing her black T-shirt with Bob Marley's face on the middle, an angel, her headphones like a halo around her neck instead of her head, her curly hair flaring out.

She stepped in front of me and stood, staring at him hard. He took a step back as his friend folded his arms across his chest.

"Leave," she said. They did. She turned to face me.

"I know them," Serine said, smiling as if to comfort me. "They bark a lot but don't bite. Bitches. That's all those two are."

"They looked a little scared when they saw you."

Serine's smile left as quickly as they had.

"They know my mother," she said. "Want me to walk you home?"

I nodded. We left and walked down White Plains Road.

"What's your name?" I asked.

"Serine."

"I recognize you," I said. "You're in my English class."

"Yup."

"Mr. Gregory is fuh-iiiine. Too much reading, though.

It's like he wants us to read every book ever written ..."
Just kept on.

After I finished my dissertation, she said, "You talk
a lot."

"Is that bad?"

Serine shook her head. I continued, switching my
commentary to which cartoons were worth my time
and why. Things I thought but never said. I never had
a receptive audience.

I kept talking until we reached the front of my apartment complex about ten minutes later. I huffed. I had
never walked that fast before. She only slowed down
when we reached corners and she had to rely on me
to know which way to turn.

"Want to come in?" I asked.

She nodded, and we went inside. I asked her if she
wanted a vanilla pudding cup. She said yes and asked
me what my name was. June, I answered, grabbing
two cups from the fridge. I handed her one of them. I
opened a drawer and grabbed two spoons.

"Want me to walk with you to school tomorrow?"
Serine asked as I gave her a spoon, following up with
an assurance that no one would bother me if she walked
with me.

"Okay," I said, ripping open my vanilla pudding cup,
my shoulders shrugging, my heart tugging. Another
save.

A YEAR AND A HALF LATER, MY MOTHER TOLD ME SHE wanted to send me away to boarding school per the suggestion of her boss, the only senior partner at her law firm who was a woman of color. She declared to me one evening, "You are going to be *her*, that's going to be *you*."

And if I was going to be *her*, asserted my mother, I had to go to private school. Not just one in the city, but one where I wouldn't live in my home. Her boss had sent her own daughter to a boarding school in upstate New York the year before. She encouraged my mother to have me apply to the same school, telling her that the school offered scholarships.

I thought the idea was mean. Like it was a legal way to give me away without giving me away. I completed the application, took the required exams, was given an interview, and was informed that I would receive their decision later on that semester.

I told Serine about the whole thing one February afternoon during our eighth-grade year in my apartment, several days before my bull escaped me. Sprawled on my couch, I yapped away. Serine sat on the carpeted floor in front of me, leaning against one of the armrests.

"She wants to get rid of me so she can have the place to herself. She probably wants to bring men home."

Serine nodded.

"She'd miss me, though. She'd miss me more than I'd miss her, I know that much. She's going to want me back," I said, nodding my head up and down like I was listening to my own sermon. "She's going to *miss me*."

"I'd miss you," Serine said, looking at me.

What would she have missed about me? My chatter? I knew I'd miss her. I didn't want to miss her. I didn't want the opportunity.

I grabbed the school's brochure from my backpack on the couch by my feet.

"No, you wouldn't, because you'd be there."

Serine didn't respond. She sang a Michael Jackson tune, "Will You Be There."

"If you apply," I continued, "you'd get in."

Serine stopped singing. Her face fell slightly.

"Ms. Lambdy loves you."

Ms. Lambdy is how Serine addressed my mother. My mother loved her for that. Her respect. Serine loved my mother too. She never told me that, but I knew. She saw the hug my mother gave me many evenings when she came home from work. One evening, I glanced at her face after my mother hugged me. Longing.

"She loves me soooo much," I said, rolling my eyes, flitting my hand in the air, personifying drama. "She wants to send me away."

"Yup."

I stared at the brochure's cover, two students walking on a pathway, surrounded by lush trees and grass. I looked back at Serine. It was the first time that I thought ahead, imagining an afternoon during the following year if I got accepted. What my day would look like without her. What her day would look like without me.

Reaching over, I dropped the brochure on her lap.

"Take it home with you. Maybe it's not too late to apply."

Serine held the brochure and read it from cover to cover. Watching her read it was like watching her daydream. Without her headphones.

THE NEXT MORNING, I MET SERINE AT OUR USUAL corner. I also met a purplish-red mark around her neck.

"What happened?"

"Nothing," she mumbled.

Serine didn't speak for the rest of the walk. Instead, she sang Billie Holiday's "Willow Weep for Me." I'd heard her sing that song before. On days when her face trembled. When she looked like she would have erupted in shouts if I wasn't there.

When I asked her nothing.

THE REST OF THAT WEEK, SERINE STILL CAME HOME with me, but we no longer watched TV. I refused to turn it on. I said very little. She offered me prompts again, and I shut them down. I even took out homework to work on in the living room, and I always saved that for after she left, after dinner later on in the evening.

Serine followed my lead, and we worked on our

algebra assignments, me with a calculator, her without one, because she didn't need it, she already had one in her head. She finished our shorter assignments before me because she worked like she walked, fast.

Since I pressed mute on myself, she listened to her music instead. Her headphones covered her ears but couldn't cover her neck. The mark. It was as if I had met Serine for the first time. I snuck peeks at it when I thought she wasn't paying attention.

I thought about the year before in seventh grade. Serine was at my apartment every weekday. The summer before we started the eighth grade, she was at my place almost every day. I offered to visit her at her home, but she always refused. The only times she ever looked angry were when I suggested hanging out at her place, wherever it was.

Days I imagined where she lived were days when she was sullen, even more quiet than usual. I would notice it but not ask about it. I didn't want to know.

My mother had always told me to mind my own business anyway when it came to other people. I had done a good job at that, especially with Serine, rarely asking her about her family because the few times I had she shut me down with phrases like *none of your business* and *nobody you'd care about*. Phrases that should've pinched my feelings but didn't.

I couldn't stop sneaking peeks at her neck. I didn't talk. By the Friday of that week, the line had almost faded. Perhaps everything would go back to normal.

Maybe I would forget that mark and recite my dissertations again. I believed that was her hope.

THE FOLLOWING MONDAY, SERINE SHOWED UP TO meet me at the corner of Boston and White Plains fifteen minutes later than usual. Her eyes were red.

"Where's your cassette player?"

"Broke it."

"Who? Not you. Your dad?"

"I never met him." We started walking. I knew she regretted telling me that.

"Was it your mother? What did she do to you?"

No response.

"I won't tell anyone," I promised.

"I know," she said.

I waited. She didn't speak. I waited for her to sing. When she didn't do that, I gave it a try. The Billie Holiday song. By then, I knew it by heart.

LATER THAT AFTERNOON, SERINE WAITED FOR ME IN the hallway by our school's exit. I reached her and looked at the open doors instead of her face.

"You can't come over today," I said.

"You have to be somewhere? I'll come with you."

"I'm going home," I said, turning my head to look at her. "We have people coming over this evening."

Serine nodded, her eyes looking downward. As if she

caught herself doing something wrong, she brought her eyes back up to mine. "I'll walk with you."

"No, I have to stop at the supermarket first. I'll see you tomorrow." I ushered myself out of there and down the stairs. I turned in the opposite direction of our usual walk. I walked around the corner of our school's building. I stood by the corner and waited.

Grateful for all the activity of students around me, I peeked back around the corner. Serine walked down the stairs. Keeping a distance of a block, I followed her to White Plains Road. Then I followed her down another street that I had never walked on before.

From a block away, I saw Serine enter a red-brick, five-story building. After waiting for a few moments, I crossed the street. I didn't wait too long. I didn't know what apartment she lived in, and she could have seen me through a window if it faced the street. I shuffled myself to the entrance and looked at names listed behind glass with black buttons next to them. I skimmed through the list and found her last name, Octavius. Next to it, 3F. I waited until someone opened the building's entrance door to leave. I held the door and entered the lobby.

I took the elevator up to the third floor. I stepped out and walked down the hall, looking for her apartment door. Yells. The low-pitched furor was from a woman. I reached her apartment door when I heard Serine's voice.

I should've pounded the red door from outside to let her know that I was there, that I was listening. I softly tapped the door with my palm as if it were her shoulder. I wanted to break in, find her and shoplift her, to quietly usher her out, to pretend that she was mine and never bring her back. All I could see was the scratched-up red door. All I heard was red.

Serine's sobs turned down from loud to soft, as if someone had turned down her voice like a stereo knob. The silence woke me from my shock.

I stepped away from the door and turned, running toward the stairway. After descending three flights of stairs, I almost pushed an elderly woman blocking the stairway entrance, looking for something in her pocketbook. I said sorry but was already outside of the building then, running across the street. I reached the lone payphone on the corner.

Grabbing the receiver, I dialed 911. I told the operator that I heard screams from my neighbor's apartment. I gave her Serine's address and apartment number. When she asked me for my information, I hung up. I stood by the phone as if it was my other best friend, and we waited for the police to show up.

After fifteen minutes, a cruiser pulled up to the building. Two officers stepped out of the car and went inside. Another fifteen minutes later, the officers returned. One was holding the arms cuffed together by the hands of a woman who had Serine's features, thin lips, round eyes. The other police officer walked with

Serine. Her left eye and cheek were bruised, making her face uneven. Her right eye caught me.

Me, with my arms folded around my chest, as if I were the one who needed protection, standing next to the payphone, no longer my partner in justice, now my partner in crime. Her right eye widened, her left eye couldn't. Her right eye narrowed at me before she turned her face away and followed the police officer to the ambulance, which had just arrived. I waited and watched all the activity.

After the police car and ambulance drove away, I understood what I had learned. And what I did. And that I loved someone other than my mother.

I WALKED DOWN BOSTON ROAD, MY BODY BARELY pushing itself forward. When I reached my apartment, I noticed our minivan resting in the driveway. I'd hoped that it would be gone. That would've been my assurance that my mother wasn't home. My whole person felt limp, and I knew that if I went in and saw my mother's face, I would've wept. She would've asked me what was wrong and I wouldn't have answered her.

Was I falling apart from seeing Serine's bloody, bruised face? Perhaps it was the look she gave me, the one that convicted me of betraying her.

SERINE WAS OUT OF SCHOOL FOR THE FOLLOWING

three weeks. My mother noticed my silence during that time. One evening after dinner during the first week Serine was gone, as we were clearing our table, my mother said, "I haven't seen your friend in some time."

No response.

"I like that girl," my mother continued. "Is she coming to visit us again soon?"

"No."

She regularly asked me about her. Until I received my acceptance letter the following week from the school in upstate New York. A full-tuition academic scholarship. Once she read that, questions about my friend ceased.

When Serine returned to school, I found her in our algebra class. Her face was no longer bruised. No headphones around her neck. She didn't sit next to me. She selected a seat in the back of the room. Our teacher must have known, or guessed, what happened to her when she didn't ask her to take her regular seat.

After class, she briskly walked out, not looking my way. I called out her name. She ignored me. Later that day when she saw me in the cafeteria walking toward her, she dropped her tray of food on the floor, turned around, and ran. As if I was going to chase and catch her. As if I was the monster.

Months later, I didn't see Serine at our graduation ceremony. Her name was called out, and when no one stepped up on the stage they skipped to the next one. When my name was announced earlier, I'd seen my mother waving her arm, smiling wide.

"That's my daughter!" she yelled over light, polite claps.

Serine was right. She did love me.

The red door. The memory left as it came, quickly, and I saw my mother's smiling face again. I saw what Serine wouldn't have seen if she had been there, what I assumed she never saw.

A week later, I returned to the red-brick building. I pressed the black button next to 3F.

After a few moments, I heard, "Who is it?"

"June Lambdy," I replied to Serine's voice as if I introduced myself to her for the first time.

She buzzed me in. I took the elevator and arrived on her floor. I reached her apartment, noticing there were no yells, no screams, no sounds at all. Just quiet. And her red door.

That's why she didn't tell me. If I didn't know about her life, I wouldn't be able to remind her. She must have thought that when I saw her, all I would've seen would've been bruises and blood.

When she opened her red door, I didn't see any of that. I saw my friend—my friend I had missed—wearing her oversized black T-shirt with Michael Jackson's face on it. A picture of his face was also in my hand, on the cover of the CD version of *Thriller*. I held it out to her, along with a packaged portable CD player.

"Cassette players are going out," I said.

Serine took them from me. "Thanks," she said.

"You could've said something."

Serine raised an eyebrow, the first skeptical look I'd ever seen her give. "What for?"

"I would've listened."

She snickered. "And then what? I would've come back here."

I had no rebuttal for that. I just stood on the other side of her open door, the side that somehow I had always stood on. I wanted to ask her questions.

Is your mother still in jail? Who's living here with you now? What's going to happen with you?

She did the asking instead. "Did you get accepted?"

"Yes," I replied, feeling too inept to lie.

"Are you going?"

"My mother's making me go."

"Good," Serine said, offering me a small smile, her own parting gift to me. "You should go home."

I wanted to ask her if she would walk with me. But she would've said no. And then what?

"See you," I said.

I turned and walked down the hall, not reaching the halfway point before I heard her red door close, locks turning.

I NEVER SAW SERINE AGAIN. IN THE EIGHT YEARS since then, I haven't invested myself in anyone. Not in any way that counts. I hang out with people, friends, acquaintances. I accept invitations and attend parties. I listen. I talk. But I don't speak. Not much. Not truly.

Not because I don't have much to say. My opinions and feelings sprout like new hairs. I just shave them off as soon as I notice them. Words can induce good change, but how often? How fully?

In the three-plus years I have known Regina, I have almost abandoned those questions, the supporting beams of my relative silence. Especially on days when she played music on her stereo in her room.

One evening last semester, I heard Billie Holiday blare from her stereo while I was studying for my physics final. It was like finding a random hundred-dollar bill in my back pocket. I never heard Billie Holiday's voice before, but I knew her lyrics, her words.

I wanted to run into her room and hug her. I wanted to tell her many things before that song ended. I still do. Especially today, when she called me this morning, asking for my thoughts. Regina's intelligent and independent, yet she openly and willingly relies on me. I should speak my mind. She deserves it.

Even so, sitting here, I remain her confidant while I don't allow her to become anything more than my activity partner.

Regina waits. As I take a piece of bread, I want to tell her what I truly think. I spread butter on my roll, knowing that I should advise her to flip a coin for it because either way, she'll be fine.

I want to tell her that if she can't flip a coin because this choice is that crucial, she should pick the free ride. I'd tell her to save the money, forget the prestige. She *is* prestige.

I won't say any of that.

Regina looks like she's going to reach across the table and shake me, playfully. I notice for the first time that her eyes look a bit like Serine's—same round shape. For a few moments, I pretend Regina is her and this is Serine's dilemma, one that could be easily addressed.

What if Regina was Serine walking toward me? What would I have said?

Other than *I'm sorry*?

I'm sorry I was clueless. I'm sorry I couldn't help her. Maybe I did with the call. Sometimes I want to know. It would be as easy as typing her name in a search engine online to see what would come up.

Yet I'm still thankful for all the days I have walked around my neighborhood during school breaks and haven't seen her curly hair, her speedy walk, her head shaking to a freeing melody playing through her headphones, only for her to see me, stop walking, yank off her headphones, and yell out, "And then what?!"

And now what? I lean back in my chair, seeing Regina again. I see from the nodding of her head that she has already decided. I also see from her eyes gluing themselves on mine that she wants me, with my words, to confirm it. My friend needs to do that—and so many things in this life—on her own.

Nevertheless, she wants me to speak.

I hum a tune and eat my bread.

Paying

YOUR MOTHER TOLD YOU THAT YOU WOULD NOT ALWAYS NEED HER, THAT YOU WOULD NOT ALWAYS NEED YOUR SIBLINGS, THAT YOU would not always need your friends. She told you this after you showed her your diamond ring.

I did it, you told her, I got engaged. She became enraged, her eyes lighting up the way your ring did, bright and blistering.

Your ring's glistening but your future isn't, she insisted.

She proceeded to tell you what you would always need. She said it as urgently as you knew she needed it.

Money. You need to make your own, she said. Your fiancé makes a lot of money but his cash won't be your cash, she said.

If he makes it, he can take it and if he can take it, he can retain it and if he retains it, he maintains you, sustains you, ultimately detains you, she said disdainfully.

I let your father make the checks but *we* didn't cash them, *he* did. He gave me what he thought was mandatory for the week, maybe for the month. I spent it on you and your sisters when I could have saved it for myself. I should have, she said.

I have the house but that's it. Who's preserving it?

Nobody. I can't afford to preserve my life, let alone this tomb I call my home.

Why tomb? you asked her. Not all your childhood memories were joyful but there must have been a smile here and there, laughter once in a while in her one-story house, you thought.

Ask your sisters why they never come to visit, she replied.

You didn't need to ask them.

Your mother left your family one time when you were six years old. She returned two days later because she had nowhere to go beyond those forty-eight hours. She described her two-day departure as subscribing to something—the first month was free, then the bills came.

Your father punched your mother often, your older sisters told you. You tried to remember those times but couldn't. Maybe wouldn't.

Your father died when you were twelve. Your mother shed tears after learning most of the money he made he had already given to a woman who claimed him as hers with the title of girlfriend but with no certificate. The love she had for your father was her entitlement, that woman maintained when your mother sought her out and asked her to pay back all those years' worth of money.

Like your mother's credit cards, that woman declined, saying to your mother, "You have his house."

Maybe your mother's house was a casket after all.

Your mother worked two part-time jobs to maintain her house at an age she would have instead retired. For years, your sisters have told her to sell it. Breathe new life into an affordable apartment, new walls where she could make new memories, where she wouldn't have to pay for much, just rent and utilities, food and toiletries.

She refused.

Sell the house, you encouraged her further, backing up your sisters who weren't there with you. Sell the house and I will matriculate into a college, you negotiated. I will earn my bachelor's degree, you said. I will produce my own money.

Twisting the diamond on your finger to face the inside of your palm, you repeated your request. You must live with your past but maybe you can sell it too, you said, get some equity. Make your own money. Make your own future.

She shook her head before shaking your hand. She pried open your fist and turned your ring back around so the diamond would show again. She stared at it, glaring at your diamond's flare.

She mumbled *sorry*. You weren't certain if the word was her decision, an apology, a description or some kind of empathy.

You wondered what drew your mother to your father in the first place. Did she agree to share her life with him because she loved him? If she loved him, what for? Maybe he promised to take care of her. Maybe he bought this coffin to peddle her that promise.

I'm marrying my fiancé because he's a good person, you told her. He made me no promises, you said. I didn't need pledges because I already observed who he was and still is, you said. I took my time to see how he treated other people, not only me.

My diamond ring, you added, is only the icing.

Your mother shrugged her shoulders and said marvelous for you, excellent of you, congratulations to you.

Then she said, make your own money *still*.

She said she had no money. She said she wouldn't be able to help pay for your wedding.

You already knew that. You were never going to ask her for that. You told her she didn't need to pay for anything.

She laughed.

I'm always paying, she said.

Maid Adrift

THE GLOSSY PICTURE OF THE SKINNY WOMAN
POSING IN A LONG BEADED WHITE GOWN, HER
FACE BRUSHED WITH ROSY BLUSH AND ANTICI-
pation, crinkles up in your clenching fist. Your fingers
wrinkle this page-wide photo you had once neatly cut
out from a bridal magazine several months ago, when
you helped your mother, Chinyelu, shop for her wedding gown, the same one in the now lifeless photo, the
same one that now no longer fits her.

You didn't want to be here. You still don't. You and
Chinyelu hadn't spoken for months before she became
engaged. After she shared her news with you over the
phone, she insisted, "Mercy, you will serve as my maid
of honor."

You didn't want to serve as anything, let alone a maid
of honor to your mother. You weren't sure if you deserved such a role, not deserved as in earned, deserved
as in *Did I do something dreadful to deserve this?*

She surprised you when she ordered you to become
this person of honor. Just three months before her engagement, you told her you no longer wanted her in
your life after she called you a name, a name you didn't
deserve.

She told you that she didn't mean it—she was only

angry with you. You knew that she did mean it, she meant it because the words flew from her face instead of fumbled. She might not mean it any longer but she meant it then, the words mean with her loathing, clean with her truth. She has spouted names at you for years. That time, that name hit a nerve in a way you couldn't fathom.

You then called her a new name: Away. Not gone, just away. Far. You didn't tell her to not call you any more names. You told her to not call you, period.

She followed through on your order until her engagement. Weddings can be nonnegotiable events, you knew then. If you refused to call her, fine. If you refused to show up at her wedding, well...not well.

Here you are, well and ready. Ten minutes ago, you gripped the stuck zipper with your thumb and pointer finger and the top button with your other hand, yanking the closed button up to help the zipper make her dress whole, Chinyelu speaking in Igbo, then switching back to English, calling out, "Please, God, help me!"

You told her in an assured whisper to calm down and breathe in. Breathe in well and deep, you ordered her. You yanked and pulled.

"You did this on purpose," she snapped.

"How? Did I pack extra pounds on your flesh?"

A tiny gasp. She didn't expect that. Not from you.

After a few quiet moments, she gave you a command. "Fix it!"

You dropped your hands at your sides, stepping back.

You inhaled, counted to ten, then exhaled, trying to ignore Chinyelu roaming around the bedroom, her arms extended behind her back, trying and failing to zip up her gown.

Fix it. As if she had asked you to pour spilled milk back into a glass. Chinyelu compared herself to milk when she first told you of her engagement to her man-friend, Ned, over the phone.

"No one drinks expired milk."

You replied, "You're not milk and you're not expired," but you knew what she meant. You wanted to chalk her comment up to society—how often do wealthy older men marry women their own ages? Not often, you assume. Youth is queen. Youth as in early twenty-somethinghood. As a thirty-five-year-old, you get that twentysomethings may not be in charge, but they are the charge. They are the pulse of all that is sought after.

Maybe *all* is melodramatic. *Most* is most accurate. Surely in this context. That's why when your mother called her upcoming wedding a miracle after calling herself expired milk, you firmly said, "No, it's not a miracle," when you secretly agreed with her.

You felt shame from thinking that. Then the shame evaporated when you realized it wasn't her age that made all of this—her upcoming marriage to a big-hearted man who asked you, her eldest child, for your blessing first—a wondrous thing.

It was her. The woman who often said destructive

things with no concern of who would be hurt if those words reached her targets.

Your target now is time. You are losing it as you find that there is not enough time to buy another dress that will fit her. Her wedding begins in thirty minutes.

Fix it. A close friend once referred to you as Dr. Auto-Repair. Whenever anything breaks down, she said, you diagnose, then you fix. She said this after you repaired her laptop and then baked brownies for her. She broke her laptop after she broke up with her boyfriend. You figured her laptop was salvageable and got to work. The brownies were for what you couldn't salvage, her heart, broken and battered.

"Don't you mean cure?" you asked. "Doctors cure, mechanics fix."

"No," she said, chewing on a brownie. "Nothing is fully curable."

That is true, you thought. That is true, you think now, as you are sitting down, the wedding gown draping over your lap. This wedding gown that fit five months ago when you purchased it, your wedding gift to your mother, putting the entire amount on your credit card. The wedding gown that you begged her to try on again two weeks ago to ensure it still fit.

The same woman who laughed away your concern and said, "Just make sure you can still fit into your bridesmaid's dress."

"Matron of honor's dress," you corrected.

"Matron? Maid," she corrected back. "You would be

my matron of honor if you had remained with Astin. You never listen."

Astin the Asset, your mother had always referred to him. Astin the Asshole, your friends always called him. Astin who punched your face when you refused to move with him to Los Angeles. Astin whom you punched back—a surprise left swing uppercut—slicing his cheek with the diamond ring you didn't return after breaking up with him by bruising his jaw.

Of course, Chinyelu didn't know about that, she still doesn't. She only knew of his smarmy charm and his mad-moneyed "mansion" in the Hamptons. She called his three-bedroom house with a large basement and a squiggly-shaped pool in the back a mansion. Perhaps his Jaguar and the term "Hamptons" made his admit-tedly remarkable house a mansion. Maybe Chinyelu just liked saying the word. Perhaps she hoped that mansion or not, his home would become yours, and maybe by some biologically entitled osmosis, hers.

Astin was your first and only, so far, shot at marriage. Chinyelu, as recently as this afternoon, has continued to shoot you with bullet points of how perfect he was, and still is, for you. You translated that into how perfect he was, and still is, for her—for her to perhaps enjoy the knowledge that her daughter would have married into prosperity.

Prosperity. Chinyelu has admitted that she is mar-rying Ned for that. His mansion—an actual man-sion—sits on acres of manicured land. Ned had pursued Chinyelu for years, through friendship-related dinners and activities. She finally considered him as a potential life partner after her car accident over a year ago. Ned dropped everything to take her to medical appointments and provide her around-the-clock care-giving. It was how he held your mother's hand during a dinner after their engagement that made you think, wow, what a wonder.

A wonder that a love like that existed and could exist for Chinyelu. You knew what she either didn't know then or could never admit—she wanted someone not to buy her jewelry or take her shopping. She wanted someone to happily hold her hand. Someone to sweetly stick around.

Security. A security protecting her heart rather than her financial future. That is the true reason Chinyelu is marrying Ned, though she doesn't show it. That is the true reason why you have not yet married anyone. The day you find a man who is kind, loyal, respectful, and sincere—who loves you for everything you are—is the day you will say yes to walking down an aisle in a strapless, silky wedding gown.

If that day never arrives, you will be alone, you know this. It will be an aloneness you will safeguard from the scrutiny of well-meaning friends, an aloneness that you will many times celebrate (mainly because you are now financially self-sufficient) but other times will snack on you, nibble at your sides, and reach your center.

Overall, you are well. You are doing well. You are

currently the chief technology officer of a top-tier investment firm. Chinyelu didn't congratulate you when you shared the news of your promotion with her three years ago. She didn't say *well done* after you explained how hard you worked and how you triumphed over the myriad of bullshit you dealt with as one of the few women and the only Black woman in your firm, working with people who tried to treat you as inferior to them.

Your mother only instructed you to not parade your awesomeness to eligible men. You were not yet fully successful, according to your mother, not until you became the chief technology officer of your own house with a husband and children. A big family with a bigger house that people could see from a far distance.

Show off. Chinyelu wanted to invite everyone she had ever met to her wedding, as her family only consists of you and your brother. Perhaps your mother was lonely growing up in Nigeria as an only child. Perhaps having no siblings and estranged in-laws (estranged since the day your father left your family many years ago) made Chinyelu hungry for other types of resources and validation. When your mother and father moved here to the States a few years before you were born, your mother might have felt even more displaced. Not having much family in general must have been tough. No longer having a home country in addition to that must have been unbearable.

Ned wanted to get married quietly in California,

where they would also honeymoon. He didn't want to invite anyone, not even his own children and their families. You didn't blame him. In fact, you thought that idea was grand. You two do your own thing, you wanted to sing to Chinyelu. Go away to California. Just go.

You realized your thoughts were selfish and petty, you only didn't want to deal with what you are dealing with now. You want only to be a well-wisher in the wings, not Dr. Auto-Repair.

Fix it. Today is not yours, you remind yourself. It's hers. Surely, she should get a pass. Her role as the woman who birthed you, berated you, fed you, stung you, pushed you down, pushed you away yet pushed you forward and farther onward, is her lifetime pass. You've tried to revoke it but failed every time. Nothing, including love, is fully curable.

Think of something.

Chinyelu comes out of the bathroom. You find that she is beautiful, looking like a stunning photograph, similar to the picture still rumpled in your closed fist. You kept this magazine photo as both a tool and keepsake, tool today, keepsake tomorrow.

Now it's trash. You throw it in the direction of the waste bin standing by the bedroom's door. You throw it hard, and you miss. It bounces off the rim and rolls a few inches away.

You return your look to Chinyelu as she stands with a towel wrapped around her, wearing her white low-heeled shoes, tiny diamonds hanging from her ears.

Before going into the bathroom, she scowled at you. You're used to seeing that glare, the one that used to scare you as a child. That look is gone. She is the one who's now afraid.

You feel an urge to hug her and tell her everything will be wonderful. A hug won't fix it, neither will your words of encouragement. You've tried those with her during other situations, and they didn't fix anything.

You look over at the ivory stole lying beside you. The stole she had planned to cover her shoulders with. You stand up, lifting her gown and placing it over your arms. You walk over to her.

"Put this back on," you say.

"For what?"

"Put this back on," you repeat, nodding your head toward the stole. "We're going to use this to cover the back."

Her glare returns. "That won't look right! Why do you want to ruin my wedding? Please, call Azu in here."

Your younger brother, Azubuike. Your brother who is good with words, but not much else. Azu, your mother's favorite child for no other reason than he is her only son. You grab your mother's cell phone and call him.

"Ma? The photographer's waiting."

"It's Mercy. The bride is requesting you."

"Why?"

"Get here now." You hang up and toss your mother's phone on the bed.

Azu arrives a few minutes later, decked out in a sharp

black tuxedo with a red tie and vest. He walks past you straight to your mother.

"Ma, what's the issue? Clock's ticking."

"My dress doesn't fit me. Your sister wants me to look disheveled."

Azu turns to look at you. "Why did you buy her a dress that doesn't fit?"

"It fit at first. This stole will cover the open space in the back."

"That won't look right," Azu says.

"He says it won't work," Chinyelu adds.

"You know what will work? You and Ned. You and Ned will work for the rest of your lives. Let me cover your back."

"I don't think you're hearing what Ma's telling you," Azu says.

"I can't hear her," you say. "Your uselessness is too loud."

Azu raises his eyebrows. You're not certain if he's surprised at what you have just said or because your mother has not yet cursed you out for speaking to him that way.

"If you want to marry that man, you will put this on. If you do not want to get married, let me know so I can leave."

Chinyelu's glare turns into a look of shock.

"You have one minute to decide. If you don't take this gown to put on, I will leave with it, and I will not come back. Sixty seconds starting from now." You start counting down from sixty, although you are ready to leave right now, place the gown in the backseat of your car, drive two hours back to your own house, change into this gown, play *Canon in Pachelbel D* on your stereo, and marry yourself to a bottle of Chardonnay.

That's what you do. Just the first part and half of the next. You turn around before the sixty seconds are up and swipe your car keys from the nightstand. You stomp out of the room with your mother's gown and walk down the long, circular stairway. You walk through the foyer and out the door, ignoring the patient photographer standing by with his equipment. You march to your car and open the front passenger door, throwing your mother's gown on the seat. Then you walk around and get in. You turn on your car's ignition and drive away, seeing in your windshield mirror your brother running after you.

If he keeps running, he would only have to run a mile. You drive to a bar that distance away. There you will have Chardonnay, if it's served. If not, some other drink. You will toast yourself as you know no one will be toasting you.

You are mad. Both meanings of the word.

You walk into the bar, a place that wants to look like a dive with wood furnishings and not-so-ironic posters but smells of pine and freshness. You order a top-shelf drink. You tell the bartender you have no money on you.

He glances at the gown you're holding.

"Bridesmaid?"

"Maid of honor," you reply.

"Bride's being unbearable?"

You almost answer yes but remind yourself that she's your mother. You nod instead.

"On the house," he says. He smacks an empty glass on the bar and pours you the drink.

"Thank you."

"My condolences. Weddings are self-congratulatory caucuses. They all should be banned."

"Not all of them are like that," you counter. "Some of them include two people getting married who actually love each other and want their family and friends to celebrate their commitment."

"That's why you're here," he says, laughing. He's not laughing with you. You gulp down the only empathy he has provided. This Chardonnay is quite good, you observe. A good year.

This past year was good. You finally have been able to build and assert your independence. You bought your own house. You've been running every morning. Your career has continued to flourish.

You learned your mother was getting remarried. That should have been the ribbon. Someone else would be responsible for taking care of her. Your brother wouldn't—he would expect you to handle it.

As you feel a buzz coming on, you realize that you are envious. Irate.

Your mother blamed you for your father leaving both of you. Of course, he wouldn't leave his son, even though he did. Sons are prized. Azu was a good kid.

You were good too. In a different way. In a way your father couldn't tolerate. The way you shielded your mother from his punches and slaps. How you struck his face with your fist that one evening. His stupor from his drinking helped you as his lack of sobriety allowed the shock of your punch to overpower him. You kept punching his face, threatening that if he hurt your mother again, you would break his jaw.

The next day he left. A victory, you declared. Your mother regarded it as a loss, her greatest one. You wanted her to thank you. To herald you as her fierce warrior, her wondrous protector.

She called you a thief, shoplifter of her contentment.

She then slapped you the way your father had slapped her. She hit your face and then your shoulders. You didn't hit her back. You scrunched your fingers into fists and folded your arms. You wanted to shout at her. You wanted to call her names. You wanted to leave.

You wanted an apology.

You still want that, but like a life partner, you might never get one. You're holding this wedding gown, but you may never wear one. Your mother found what you are still looking for, what you will not admit you want—someone who would appreciate you, celebrate you, prioritize you.

You want another glass. You look over to the bartender. "Another one, please."

"Next one, you'll need to pay," he says.

You look down at the gown, knowing you can't provide it as payment. You realize you are lost and you have lost. You must go back.

"Is water free?"

"Not bottled," he replies. He pours tap water into a glass. He sets it on the bar, then walks away to tend to another customer.

You gulp down the water and wait. You hoist the gown over your shoulder and go to the bathroom. You can feel glances from other patrons in the bar. You welcome them. A little attention means a lot to you today.

You return to the house with the gown over your shoulder. Azu's standing by the door. You're not surprised when he says nothing to you.

You shrug. You have returned with the gown, and you are now ready to reason with the bride. You walk upstairs, back to the room you assume your mother's still waiting in. Azu follows you.

She's standing in the middle of the room. She looks at you with those eyes of hers, but for the first time, they're unrecognizable. You can't tell what she's thinking or feeling. You don't want to know. You still care to know.

Azu walks over to your mother and stands by her. You straighten your shoulders.

"This gown looks good now, doesn't it?"

As Azu sees the severity in your narrowed eyes, he also sees—you guess—the big picture. He turns to Chinyelu.

"People are waiting at the church right now," Azu says to your mother. "If you choose to get married another day, they might not attend the next time."

Chinyelu looks at both of you, then at the gown. She walks toward you and takes it from you. She retreats to the bathroom with it. Your shoulders relax. You remind yourself why you wanted to say no when your mother ordered you to serve as her maid of honor. You two are adrift.

"You'll get to be a bride one day," Azu says. "Don't take it out on Ma because that day isn't today."

"I didn't hear you. Your uselessness is still too loud."

"Smile in those pictures, Mercy. Today is not about you."

Azu leaves. You grab the stole and wait. The bathroom door opens, and your mother emerges, wearing the gown loosely. She walks to you and turns around. Her back faces you. You stuff the stole down the back and fold it out evenly. You let the stole fall towards the floor and it stops right at the end of her gown.

"Your back is covered," you announce.

Chinyelu turns around. She looks stunning. You feel warm.

"You look beautiful," you say.

"You should have asked me to try it on again before today," she snips.

"I didn't ask," you snip back, the warmth leaving you as if it's shooting out a just-opened window. "I *begged*."

Chinyelu raises her head in that indignant style, acknowledging you are right without words to confirm it.

"You left," she says.

"I did."

"Selfish."

"Yes."

Your mother waits for you to say something more. Perhaps an apology.

"I don't feel sorry," you say, realizing today will be the last day you will stand by her side.

Azu will walk your stunning mother down the aisle, but you are the one who will give her away. When you congratulate her and Ned later today, you will tell Ned, while looking straight at Chinyelu, the words flying from your face: "She's yours."

Yours. Today is not. Tomorrow will be.

Chinyelu is undaunted, you notice. She doesn't need your apology. She already has what she wants. She's ready to flaunt her figure and, most fittingly, her future in front of everyone at the church.

"Come, I must arrive on time," she says.

"We're already late," you say, grabbing her bouquet

of white roses and yours of daisies from the nightstand. Holding both bouquets, one in each hand with firm grips, you follow her lead out of the room, kicking the crumpled magazine page like a soccer ball toward a goal on the way out.

Text Me a Photo

'M PISSED THAT I MISSED YOUR CALL. I'M STILL IN SHOCK. I'M SCARING YOUR STEPDAD. ARTHUR TELLS ME TO CALL YOU ALL THE TIME. HE WANTS US TO solve this. That's the mathematician in him.

Arthur says you called not for money but to reconcile. I love my optimist, but he won't admit to me that he knows that you, my demanding, deceiving diva, are an opportunist. That's all I'm good for now. A few thousand dollars.

Arthur cut a check to send to you. Like the doctor cut you from me when you were born. Like you cut me out of your life. I should just write you an e-mail. But you need to hear me. Hear my voice when I tell you that I cut up Arthur's check.

I don't believe you when you say that you need it for your newborn. I didn't know you were expecting. You didn't even mention his name.

Text me a photo. Let me see his eyes, let me see that they are your eyes, that they are mine. Maybe it's your love for your son that made you call me. That's what happens when you love somebody more than your own self. Your pride slides, it glides, it rides away.

Because of your boy, you now know that I still love you, even though I can't stand you. I can't stand not seeing you, not knowing where you are. Where are you now, anyway?

Arthur! Damn. He just poured out the rest of the Merlot. It's the bottle your stepbrother gave Arthur and me last Christmas. He told us to save it for a special occasion, and I did. I opened the bottle right after hearing your voicemail this morning.

What was I celebrating? Your call? Or that I'm now a grandmother? Finally! It's about time you gave me a grandchild. You owe me that. You owe me everything. More than you will eh-vaaaah know. You'll see. You'll see after you raise your child. Year after year, your vision will clear. You will hate me less. You'll be grateful—

Arthur here. Your mom will call you back tomorrow—

Stay out of this. And don't ever pour away my good liquor again.

Listen. I prayed to God yesterday to hear your voice again. Remember when we used to sing together at night before you went to sleep? You soprano and me alto? Harmony.

Remember that hymn I taught you? You sang it in church that Christmas Eve service when you were seven. Your voice was beautiful. A bit flat. But beautiful still. Sing it to your son when he cries. That hymn will help.

Arthur and I will help. But we won't send you a check. Text me his photo. Then send us the bill. We will pay it directly.

Flight in Transit

ELDRIN'S FATHER ONCE TOLD HIM THAT IN ORDER TO FLY UP, ONE MUST FALL FIRST. HE THOUGHT HIS FATHER REFERRED TO LIVING A Christian life, humbling himself so that God could lift him up. Eldrin realized that his father might not have been talking about God. He came across this epiphany traveling from the Bronx down to Manhattan's Upper West Side, sitting on a downtown number two train.

Eldrin told his mother that morning that he was going to the library after school. He figured if he went to a branch in the Upper West Side, it wouldn't be a lie. His mother asked him to pick up a book for her. Her request was strange. To his knowledge, she didn't read anything but tabloid magazines.

"Please get me *Their Eyes Were Watching God*. By Zora Neale Hurston," his mother told him that morning. "Do you need to write it down?"

Eldrin shook his head. "Nope," he said. "Hurston. I won't forget."

He spent much time at the library four blocks away from his apartment in the Bronx, browsing comic books and graphic novels. He would endeavor to do the same, along with picking up his mother's requested book at the branch ten blocks away from his father's new apartment, after his visit.

Eldrin kept a watchful eye for Ninety-Sixth Street. He daydreamed between stations about the graphic novel series he was currently reading, *The Flame Fifteen*. They were fifteen people burned by magical fires that gave them powers to be utilized for good. Eldrin's favorite was Heartsift, the youngest, the most overlooked, the least appreciated. At fourteen, she had a vast intellect. She also had a somewhat intolerable weakness of looking for the best in everyone, even her enemies. That, with her age, made her fellow powered teammates dismiss her, rarely calling upon her to participate in battle. Eldrin had a crush on Heartsift, daydreamed about her often, all the different animations of her face smiling at him with sincere understanding.

Heartsift disappeared when the train arrived at Ninety-Sixth Street. He noticed the faces of the people who surrounded him on the train, sitting and standing. All of the faces, like his own, were somber.

AFTER LEAVING THE SUBWAY STATION, ELDRIN LOOKED up at the green-and-white street signs on the corner, the intersection of one street versus another, turned himself in a direction, and walked. Before his trip downtown, he'd researched the lined streets on a map, Amsterdam, Broadway, Columbus, Riverside, and knew which way was east and west.

Eldrin thought about how Heartsift conducted similar research before her trip in the twenty-ninth issue of *The Flame Fifteen* he had read in his bedroom the night before. One of the Fifteen, Repeeri, had gone rogue to damage an entire town, but his reasons were unknown. The head of the Flame Fifteen sent Heartsift to confront him. Heartsift was a mind reader but could also read the intentions of one's being. She would speak with Repeeri to read his heart to find out why he'd destroyed the town.

Following her journey to his location, which consisted of one page of her flying in the air, her thoughts written in a text box on top, Eldrin became inspired. Lying on his bed, the novel resting on his chest, he decided that he would do the same.

His daydream ended once again, and he found himself standing in front of the building. It had a green awning with three numbers emblazoned in gold that matched the numbers of his father's new address. The first entrance door opened to small area that had buttons next to numbers and letters, the building's apartments. Eldrin knew which one to press, but before he raised his hand, he noticed the next door of clear glass leading to the main lobby was slightly ajar. He walked in and found an attendant sitting behind a counter that looked like marble. Eldrin walked past him toward one of the two elevators ahead.

"Excuse me," the attendant called. Eldrin stopped walking and turned his head.

"Who are you here to see?"

"My dad," Eldrin replied.

"Your father's name?"

"Marlin Tynner."

The attendant picked up a phone and pressed a button. He waited and said, "You have a visitor here. He says he's your son." The attendant waited, nodded, and placed the phone down.

"You can go ahead," the attendant said.

"Thanks," Eldrin mumbled as he continued to walk. He briefly thought about his apartment building back in the Bronx, one burgundy-bricked building matching a set of several buildings standing together. How there was no one in his lobby to make calls to people who lived there. How no one would have stopped him to ask him who he was. Eldrin wondered with irritation why the attendant stopped him—did he also stop all the other visitors?

Eldrin also wondered what he would have heard if he stopped to press his father's apartment button first, the tone of his father's response when Eldrin would have said, "It's me."

Marlin opened the door. He was stocky and muscular. Eldrin saw himself looking at him, the same brown shade of skin, the same facial features, almost the same of everything, except the muscles. He didn't have those yet. At thirteen, he was almost his father's height. Shorter by three inches.

"How do you know where I live?"

"I saw your return address on the envelope you sent." An envelope they had received from Marlin three days before, containing a check for one thousand dollars made out to his mother. She called it a cheap severance package. Eldrin thought one thousand dollars was a lot of money.

Marlin nodded slowly. "Right, yes." He stepped away from the door to open it farther. Eldrin entered and saw what he never did at his own home, his father's former place of residence. Lots of open space.

A large rectangular window took up one wall on the far end of the living room. On the side was a gray couch that had thin black cushions supported by a silver frame. A glass coffee table kept the couch company.

On top of the couch on the wall were the only framed things he saw in the living room. His father's diplomas. One was his bachelor's degree and the other one was his master's degree. The master's degree was brand new. His father received that the day after he moved out. Marlin referred to it as his "MBA," standing not for his business education but for "My Best Accomplishment." Marlin said this to him later that day on the phone after Eldrin asked if he could look at the diploma sometime.

He called his father's cell phone a few times from a payphone across the street from his school late that afternoon, one of the few payphones he knew still existed. It seemed almost extraterrestrial to Eldrin. That afternoon, he looked at the payphone as if it were a spaceship, as if it were something that could transport him to someone who seemed to be a universe away, instead of a borough away.

Eldrin inserted two quarters and dialed his father's number. Marlin had just left his graduation ceremony in Manhattan when he answered his cell phone on the third beep. Eldrin heard something in his father's voice that he had never heard from him before.

Joy. He wanted to transfer it through the receiver into his ear and down to his chest. He wasn't sure what Marlin was more elated about, graduating with his master's degree or leaving their apartment for good the day before.

"Your father thinks he's too special for us now," his mother said to him that morning before the ceremony, the first morning after Marlin moved out, after Eldrin expressed his intention to go. Her eyes red with wine-facilitated exhaustion, she told him to go to school instead.

Eldrin wondered, after seeing his father's latest diploma on the wall, if Marlin was alone that day, if anyone else had come to his ceremony to support him. He thought probably not. He didn't believe his father had many friends, if he had any. Or maybe he did have friends and Eldrin didn't know them, like his father had superpowers of his own and was a part of a secret group.

Maybe his father was indeed special, dangerously so. Maybe that's why he truly left, to protect them rather than hurt them. Eldrin shook his head, shaking off the sugar from that candied illusion.

His father shut his apartment door and locked it. Marlin took one of Eldrin's backpack straps from his shoulder and Eldrin assisted, shrugging off the other strap. Marlin placed it on a tall table stand by the closed door.

"I thought I was picking you up on Saturday. I was going to take you to see that new movie that came out, the one about the superhero."

"Which one? There are three of them out."

Marlin shrugged. "Doesn't matter. Whichever one you want to see."

"I've seen all of them."

Eldrin didn't want to wait until the weekend to ask him the question to his face, even though he already had an educational guess of what his answer would be. He saw why Marlin had moved out. The open space, free of clutter, free of reminders of the persons he'd left. The quiet. No demanding cries from a woman who wanted love that he didn't want to give.

Eldrin thought his father's answer would also explain why Marlin had never married his mother. He hoped that his father would say the words, giving Eldrin a gift of confirmation. Saying it out loud would have burned him, but that burn would have closed his open wound, killing any infection of pretense.

"You need to go home, Eldrin. Is there an emergency?"

Eldrin thought to answer yes. When his father had moved out the week before, their apartment looked more or less the same, but it felt different. It felt hot, like the place was on fire. His mother yelled and cried as if flames rose around her. Eldrin couldn't put them out. He didn't know how.

He had known that fire was coming. His father worked a full-time job during the day and went to business school at night. He earned enough at his day job in Manhattan to help take care of the three of them, but the extra degree would bring him more money. Enough to take care of them without living with them.

Eldrin wanted to see if he was wrong. Perhaps he'd missed something.

He pictured Heartsift standing next to him, holding his hand, transferring her power to him through her fingers.

"Why did you move out?"

Eldrin looked at Marlin and waited for it. It was what his father's whole being yelled at him.

I want a new life!

"Come on," his father said, sighing as he shook his head.

Without your mother.

"I'll walk you to the subway," Marlin said, grabbing his son's backpack from the stand. Eldrin's neck and shoulders stiffened as he read something extra he didn't expect.

Without you.

"I'm good," Eldrin said, relaxing his shoulders, snatching his backpack from Marlin. "I can walk by myself."

"Tell your mother I'll send another check soon," Marlin said.

"You tell her," Eldrin mumbled as he placed the backpack around his shoulders and turned toward the door. He left the apartment, hoping his father would scold him on his way out.

"See you on Saturday," Marlin said as he closed the door.

Instead of walking down the hall, Eldrin stood in front of the closed door, wondering if he would kick it down with his right foot or knock it down with his clenched fists.

His shoulders slumped. All he could do was walk away.

ELDRIN STOOD ON THE PLATFORM, WAITING. RUSH hour was over, and people slowly strolled past him. He thought of his father waiting downstairs in front of their building that weekend. Perhaps he would travel up to their floor and knock on their apartment door. Would his mother answer?

His mother. Eldrin switched his thoughts to what he would say to her upon his return. She would ask for the book she'd requested that morning. He remembered the title and author. He remembered how he'd planned to ask a librarian to help him locate the book, since he had never read it before. He remembered how he'd planned to hand the book to his mother with a hug, knowing she needed that just as much as the book.

He forgot to go to the library.

He looked at his empty hands, knowing he would tell her the truth. That he had visited his father at his new apartment on Ninety-Sixth Street. He would apologize to her and endure her chastisement. She would call him no-good.

"Just like your father," she would mutter.

Eldrin heard a beep signaling the train's arrival. He closed his eyes, imagining himself becoming a flame, burning but not disintegrating, his own Heartsift, empowered.

He opened his eyes and found the Bronx-bound train, doors opening in front of him to enter. He kept still, and the doors closed shut. The train shuttled out of the station, and Eldrin stood, seeing himself flying, waiting for another train to arrive.

Carry-On

FOR THE FIRST TIME IN HER FORTY-NINE YEARS, EDWINA TRAVELED LIGHT. SHE DIDN'T NEED TO GO TO THE BAGGAGE CLAIM WHEN SHE ARRIVED at JFK. Her only carry-on was her daughter's red leather purse, which looked more like a miniature, crumpled tote bag. Its body resembled two red rosebuds fused together like conjoined twins. Her daughter once claimed that the bag had gone out of style. Edwina defended it, claiming the bag's sentimental value made it worth keeping.

"You carried it around for years like it was the *thing*," Edwina said to Bernie as she packed up her daughter's stuff two years ago, just before she moved out.

"I've outgrown it," Bernie said. "You hold on to it."

Edwina did. Stepping onto an escalator, she held the strap with her right hand, her fingers clenched into a fist. Edwina loosened her hold to allow her blood to circulate. Once her hand had feeling again, she tightened her grip, waiting for the numbness to return.

Edwina walked out of the crowded airport, ignoring the yellow cabs waiting in line, knowing that if she looked at one for too long she would vomit. Instead, she looked for the shuttle that would take her to the subway station.

"You're not a New Yorker until you've taken a cab in Manhattan, Mom," Bernie told Edwina over the phone, one month into living in the city. "It's like magic—the way they ride through the streets."

Edwina never told her that she had lived in New York City during her early twenties in the early eighties. "You're not a New Yorker until you've cursed somebody out for pinching your ass on the subway," she almost responded, but decided against it, not wanting to dampen Bernie's wonder.

As Edwina contemplated whether or not she would see her only child's face during her stay in New York, she realized that she should have told her. She should have popped that bubble.

THE TRAINS WERE DIFFERENT NOW THAN FROM HER time in New York. Silver and smooth. Electric signage. Back in her day, they were red and graffiti-laden. There were some things, Edwina noticed, that were the same.

People—serious, pensive, sleeping. Trash—present on the ground, as if crumpled bags and candy wrappers were additional passengers sitting below the seats. Edwina felt like the empty coffee cup rolling beneath the seat of the napping man across from her. She was just there, rolling along, her futility exposed.

Edwina should have been on this train last Christmas. She would have made these observations if she had traveled to New York then, when Bernie had asked her to. But then again, Bernie would have picked her up from the airport, and they would have taken a cab instead.

Bernie told Edwina that if she visited for the holidays, she would meet her at the airport with a shout and open arms. Edwina agreed to come but cancelled last-minute. Visiting Bernie last Christmas, her first Christmas as a married woman, would have been Edwina's full admission that Bernie now belonged with someone else.

Of course, Edwina didn't tell her all that. With a healthy body temperature, she told her daughter that she had the flu. And she couldn't bear the idea of getting her sick. Maybe next year, Bernie said in response. Next year.

EDWINA WAS SUPPOSED TO GET OFF AT 145TH STREET. Instead, she got off at 125th. She stepped onto the platform and tried to recall what she knew of the station, but couldn't remember what it had looked like twentysomething years before.

During her last conversation with her daughter just a week beforehand, she learned that Bernie was going to put her hair in extensions again. Bernie was impressed by the number of hair braiding salons in New York, especially in Harlem around 125th Street.

Edwina had braided her daughter's hair throughout her childhood and beyond. Edwina especially enjoyed doing it after Bernie went to college an hour's distance away from her. It was one of the few times that she was able to sit her daughter in one place for several hours, when she couldn't be distracted with her friends or schoolwork.

Bernie's hair always took time to do, and for that, Edwina was grateful. She enjoyed feeling the texture of her daughter's hair, curly and thick. She had to work to comb it out, to flatten it enough to weave in the synthetic hair. Her daughter's hair gave Edwina more time when it seemed to be disappearing with every year that Bernie got older and became more self-sufficient.

Edwina offered to come out to New York during that phone conversation. "I'll come and braid your hair," she said to Bernie, only eight days before.

"You're not going to come here for that," Bernie said. "When you visit, I just want you to hang out with Melvin and me. We would love to have you."

Thinking of her daughter's words, Edwina also thought that maybe she would decide to see Bernie.

How did her braids turn out? Were they thinner than the braids Edwina had done? Did they frame her face well?

ONE HUNDRED THIRTY-FIFTH STREET. TEN BLOCKS of walking, and Edwina grew tired. She wanted to sit down somewhere and rest. Perhaps she would return to the subway. The 135th subway stop was in front of her. Perhaps she would enter the station and take two trains back to Queens, where she would hop on a shuttle that would take her to the airport. She would purchase a seat on the next flight back to Seattle. The thought of that option appealed to her as much as a cushioned seat.

Edwina shook her head. She opened Bernie's bag and looked at her shut cell phone. She knew that her voice mailbox was most likely full. Perhaps it was a good time to listen to her messages.

No. Not yet.

A good three or four of those messages were most likely from her best friend, Amelia. Good friend Amelia. The only one who tried to reach her beyond a phone call. The only one who showed up at Edwina's apartment door two days before.

"Eddie!" *Knock, knock, knock.* "I know you're home. Let me in."

Horizontal on her living room couch, her arms at her sides, Edwina's wine-stained eyes blinked away tears.

Leave, she wanted to say at a volume level Amelia couldn't hear. Return to your husband at your big house full of yellow tulips, open windows, and smiling photos of your three grown children and seven grandchildren. Go home and let me be.

Amelia did go home. Then she returned. Five times back and forth throughout those two days before Edwina had taken her flight to New York. Edwina thought maybe Amelia had camped outside of her apartment in the hallway for a few hours each time, hoping to catch her sneaking out. Edwina waited her out. She knew she could. Amelia had a family who needed her.

No one would be waiting for Edwina to return to her apartment after she left. And while someone was now waiting for her in New York, it was not the same.

There were other people waiting for her too. Waiting for her to call them back. Edwina wanted only one person to call. She wanted to hear only one voice. Edwina knew she wouldn't hear her voice ever again.

ONE HUNDRED FORTIETH STREET AND BROADWAY. The building perched on top of the liquor store was the same as it was twenty years ago. The entrance to the apartment building was different than before. It was black now, red then. Twenty-six years ago, she conceived Bernie in that building, inside an apartment on the second floor.

Bernie's father. His studio apartment resembled a different kind of studio, a musical one with a band full of instruments. He played the piano, the flute, the saxophone. He was also a trombone player, a guitar player, and a lady player. Out of all instruments, he played the woman the best.

Edwina knew she wanted him as soon as she met him at that liquor store next door. He stood by the counter, smoking a cigar, holding his bottle of brandy with conviction. She gave him a pickup line: "Want to share that bottle?" It worked.

There was something about him that Edwina desired. Perhaps it was his sense of ownership. His life was not the most fruitful, but he owned it. Edwina longed to own something, even if it wasn't something good.

Any song Edwina wanted to hear, he played it. Any promise that she wanted from him, he said it. It was all fantasy and bullshit, she knew it and wasn't concerned. She was twenty-three and family-free. No parents, no siblings. She was okay with that. She hoped to never get married, to never have children. She wanted to be as free as her musician, with neither anchors nor regrets.

She thought she could capture his essence through her arms and legs, that maybe if she joined her body with his, she could join his life with hers and then she would become him. Free.

She didn't get free. She got a globe-shaped tummy.

Her wants changed shape along with her stomach. Perhaps she wanted a family of her own after all, but thought she never would have one.

Edwina proposed. Marry me, she pleaded to her musician. We can do this. You and me, baby makes three and music makes four. No, he said. You'll live for you. I'll live for me.

He no longer sang her songs. He no longer played for her. Five months into her pregnancy, she said good-bye to her musician and to New York.

Edwina wondered if he still lived in that building

on the second floor. Maybe she had just walked past him on the street. Maybe Bernie during her time in New York had met him without knowing who he was.

Bernie seemed content growing up without a father, as she made Edwina's life as a single parent easier than expected. Bernie asserted her independence from an early age, she potty-trained herself at two, started saving money from her first cash gift at six, started cooking her own meals at ten. Long-term planning was Bernie's specialty. At twelve, she started encouraging Edwina to date.

"You should try to find someone, Mommy," Bernie said, as if she knew something that Edwina didn't know or couldn't foresee. Edwina did see men from time to time. No one lasted more than several months. They all had one nonnegotiable thing in common—they didn't want Edwina as much as she wanted them. She didn't want her daughter to share the same fate, ending up with someone and still feeling unwanted.

She got her wish. Her daughter fell in love with Melvin, a man who not only wanted her but also loved and respected her. Proposed to her only after he asked for Edwina's permission and blessing first. Came from a caring family who treated Bernie well.

After the wedding, Melvin wanted to move to New York to start his law career. And, of course, he wanted to bring his wife with him. Had he shared his plan before he asked Edwina for her daughter's hand in marriage, Edwina wouldn't have given her permission and blessing. She would have said, simply yet sternly, *no*.

You can only have my daughter if she is a few miles away, only if she is reachable, she would have told Melvin. She is all I have, Edwina would have implored him, her eyes bearing her desperation.

Single parenting had its challenges, but Edwina had no idea how much tougher it would be when her daughter got older, when she got grown, when her parenting work was no longer work of daily joyfulness and monotony. Edwina's work had become quieter—hopes of her daughter's everyday well-being wished in the silence of her own loneliness. Even though she longed to have a spouse, she didn't know how much more she would want that until her daughter found her own partner.

"Be brave," Amelia coaxed her over the phone, almost two years back, right before Bernie moved east with Melvin. "We don't have children to keep them forever, Eddie."

"Simple for you to say that. I only have my one," Edwina countered. "Who is he to take her away that far?"

"He's her husband."

"I'm her mother."

"I understand," Amelia said. "Listen, I love all my children. I would die for all of them. But I have a favorite, and—"

"You're not supposed to have favorites," Edwina admonished.

"Simple for you to say, Eddie," Amelia said. "You only have your one."

"Who's your favorite then? I'd guess Cheryl."

Out of all three of Amelia's children, Cheryl gave her the most bragging currency. She was the second oldest but the first to give Amelia grandchildren, the first to graduate with an advanced degree, the first to buy a house. Amelia could talk for thirty minutes about Cheryl's work as a professor, her publications, her four gorgeous children, her handsome, successful, and devoted husband.

"No," Amelia said. "Keith."

Keith was the youngest, born five years after Cheryl. He dropped out of college, had yet to move out of the house, and for most of his young adulthood had no ambition beyond getting front-row tickets to concerts.

"He's kind to me. We have real conversations. He's the only one who remembers my birthday. Now I'm losing him. To Sheila."

"I thought you liked Sheila."

"I do. She's the reason why he's back in school. She's making him grow up. That's great, but they're serious. Keith told me he wants to marry her soon. After my two oldest were married, I barely saw them. They rarely visited. They still don't. Only on holidays, really, and now Devin and I have two sets of in-laws to compete with for their time. But even then, that isn't so bad for me, because as much as I love Cheryl and Martin,

I don't enjoy their company much. Sounds shameful, doesn't it?"

"More like honest," Edwina replied. "And heart-breaking."

"Yes, very," Amelia agreed. "Bernadette is moving to New York—so what? She'll still call you every day, and when she does, you'll hear her worship of you in her voice. Cheryl lives only ten minutes away from me, and I don't see her often. When I do, she talks to me like she's doing me a favor. Sometimes I wish that she would move to another state, maybe even the East Coast. It would be easier to tolerate her. Physical distance is always better than emotional, trust me."

Edwina shook her head. As if Amelia could see her quiet dissent over the phone, she continued, "The way she looks at you, the way her voice rings when she addresses you—I wish Cheryl would see me and talk to me that way. I envy you, Eddie. Your daughter adores you."

"Stop talking nonsense," Edwina chided. "Cheryl loves you."

"She loves me because she's obliged as my daughter. One is never obliged to adore anyone."

EDWINA REACHED 145TH STREET. SHE SAW BERNIE'S husband, tall, handsome, and morose, standing on the corner by a building with a green awning, where a black, rectangular box-shaped car waited out front.

She wanted to slap him. For marrying Bernie. For taking a law firm job in Manhattan instead of Seattle. It should have been Bernie who greeted her instead. She would have had her arms wide open.

Melvin couldn't have known that a cab would strike Bernie on her way to a dinner party downtown. He couldn't have known that his wife would jaywalk on a busy street with large parked cars that made blind spots for other cars making turns. Melvin couldn't have predicted that, yet Edwina still wanted to slap him.

"We waited for you as long as we could," Melvin said. "I left you voicemails. I thought you would get here before the wake started."

"Missed my flight," Edwina said. *On purpose*, she didn't add.

"Where are your things?"

"Left them back home."

"I asked the driver to wait for you before he left," he said. "If you want, they can bring the casket back inside, if you want to view her body."

Edwina looked at the hearse, wondering how her daughter's braids looked. She'd known this moment would come. She chose. She chose to not see Bernie's face.

"No. And I'm not going with you to the cemetery. I'd rather stay behind at your place. I'd like to sort through some of her things, be that annoying mother I haven't been since she married you."

"You have to be at the burial," Melvin said, softly

placing his hand on her shoulder, the same way Bernie had when she wanted to comfort her. Edwina jerked her shoulder away and slapped his cheek.

"I don't have to be anywhere," she snapped. "Tell the driver to go ahead."

Melvin's face was blank, as if he hadn't felt any sting from Edwina's palm. He must also be numb, Edwina sensed as he stepped away to speak with the driver. After a few moments, the driver nodded, entered the hearse, and drove away. Edwina watched the car roll along until it made a right turn at a traffic light and disappeared.

As her son-in-law walked back toward her, Edwina looked down, noticing Bernie's red-rose bag lying on the ground. She knelt down to collect it, cursing herself for letting it drop.

Bars

YOU LOOK INSIDE YOUR BLUE BACKPACK TO MAKE SURE YOU HAVE EVERYTHING. YOUR REPORT CARD IS NEATLY WEDGED BETWEEN your class picture and the book you're currently reading. It's the fourth installment of a series of books about a young detective. The other three books you own from that series are placed in the other zipped compartment of your bag. You dream of becoming a sleuth one day, solving the mysteries of other people.

You look up at your aunt, a young woman named Isabel, whose cocoa-brown eyes complement her long braids. She is wearing a black pea coat and a blue cashmere sweater, with her long black skirt draping over her black leather boots. She is royally confident, effortlessly stunning.

"I'm ready," you tell her.

Aunty Isabel smiles. "Good. Shall we, Mademoiselle?"

You nod, and the two of you leave her apartment. You smile because you love it when she calls you *Mademoiselle*. Makes you feel taller.

AFTER YOU AND YOUR AUNT LEAVE THE BUILDING, THE two of you walk toward the corner of the street. The frigid air makes you relieved that your aunt made you wear two layers of clothes instead of one. Your black bubble-goose jacket and yellow ski cap make you look like a giant penguin. Your walk is more like a waddle because you find it hard to keep a cool stride as you are wearing jeans, heavy stockings, and chunky boots.

A black car waits at the corner. Her boyfriend, whom you call Uncle Reuben, is waiting in the driver's seat. He rolls down the front passenger window and waves to you. You wave back as Aunty Isabel opens a backseat door for you to enter his car. She takes the front.

"Make sure you buckle up," she instructs you. You do as she says, making sure your seat belt is properly latched.

"Buckled!" you alert, as if you are on your way to your favorite toy shop or, better yet, your beloved bookstore.

You all drive off, and the voyage begins. You take off your gloves and clasp your fingers together to keep them from twitching and twirling, knowing that you will soon reach your destination, where your reward awaits.

You arrive at a parking lot filled with other cars and buses and people bustling all over.

You and Aunty Isabel leave Uncle Reuben's car. You say good-bye to him.

The two of you make your way to the line of mostly women and children waiting to step up on a bus. Your fingers are acting up again because they know that you are getting much closer. It has been too long since you have won last. You have been waiting for a long time.

Five months. Eleven days.

Aunty Isabel gently squeezes your hand. "We're almost there," she says.

You two step up onto the bus and choose two seats at the back, with you by the window and your aunt right next to you. You remove your backpack from your back and hold it close to your chest. After a short while, the bus drives off the lot and makes its way onto a bridge that crosses over a huge stream of water. You wonder if it's the Atlantic Ocean or just some wide river. The sun reveals the crystals sprinkled on the surface. You feel like swimming. You think of the last time you frolicked in a pool. It was June. A few weeks before the—using Aunty Isabel's special word for it—*incident*.

The *incident* that made your gift disappear, with the help of blue uniforms and silver badges.

You want to return to happy thoughts.

You now think about the main character from your favorite book series, picturing you're a fellow detective. You're answering everyone's questions, holding a magnifying glass, smoking a pipe that tastes like bubble gum.

THE SPACE REMINDS YOU OF YOUR CAFETERIA AT school, huge and colorless. There are children spread about, kids older than you, some younger. Dressed in bright orange V-neck shirts and matching pants, women are smiling, talking with their children. A few men in gray uniforms with collared shirts and thick black belts are keeping watch. Your beautiful princess is yelling at one of the uniformed watchmen, pointing her manicured finger at him.

Twenty minutes earlier, you two had arrived at this large room with the other children and supervising adults. Both of you had waited quietly by one of the long tables for one woman in particular to walk up to you with big, open eyes and greet you with a tight hug.

Aunty Isabel's patience had been drifting away, bit by bit, when she approached one of the watchmen to ask what was going on. Now her patience is disappearing altogether, chunk by chunk.

"What do you mean she's been moved upstate?"

"She was transferred this morning."

"Someone should have called me," your aunt says. "Your office *knew* we were coming."

"This happens all the time. Not our call," the uniformed man counters. "Sorry."

Your detective skills inform you that he is not sorry. He is bored and bothered.

Aunty Isabel turns her face toward you. You know what she wants to say. And you know she doesn't need to say it. As you grab your backpack and sling it over your shoulder, you tell yourself what your aunt has told you throughout this past year, many times.

Tears solve nothing.

The Glowing Conqueror

I.

She once thought she was born from a fairy tale. Rather hoped. She hoped so much that her hope became a belief, though brief. She wasn't sure which fairy tale, none of the princesses looked like her, she couldn't find her brown skin and textured black hair in any of the pages in her books.

Perhaps she was a villain. None of the villains looked like her either. She didn't have eyes green with envy, her skin was not scraggly as the ladies conniving to destroy the ivory-skinned princesses.

She was someone in between, someone in need of saving, someone in need to conquer. She wanted to be rescued by a prince. She wanted to take over like a fiendish sorceress; the one-bedroom apartment smelling of cigarettes would have been her kingdom. Perhaps not the entire apartment. More like the corner of the living room where her picture books resided, stacked against the wall. This corner, she would rule. Just like the corner of the street where her mother ruled. There, her mother was queen.

So maybe she was a princess. A princess of some-where, not the corner of that street where she lived. Maybe not even the corner of the living room. Maybe somewhere unseen. What could be seen was the color her skin glowed, matching the sky when it was day. The glow looked like icing on her eighth birthday cake, presented to her the previous week. The cake was her mother's *I'm sorry*. Usually, those gifts were given as cupcakes wrapped in plastic she would buy from the corner store. The corner store that was on the *other* cor-ner, the one where people gossiped about the queen and her tyranny down the street. How she called the shots.

This cake wasn't presented in plastic. It was brought with a box. One that looked fancy. Cream-colored, with gold circles on top. She felt special when her mother walked to the corner of the living room and sat down on the floor in front of the princess. The princess felt like her mother, like a queen, her mother temporarily becoming one of her subjects. The cake was an offering. Please forgive. And if you can, please forget.

The princess smiled. The queen tried. She always did.

No candles were needed because the princess glowed blue so bright that she was her own candle. The queen didn't seem to notice. The princess was confused.

"Can't you see me?" the princess asked.

"I always see you," answered the queen.

"I'm a light," the princess said. "I'm a blue light."

The queen smiled and nodded. "Read," she commanded, no longer sounding like a subject. "Read your books."

Her mother stood up and walked over to the front door and opened it. A tall man with matted black hair entered the apartment and grabbed the queen's waist.

"You got it for me?" he asked the queen.

The queen nodded and took his hand, leading him to the bedroom. The princess turned her attention back to her glowing skin, looking at her glazed arms, realizing while she was shining, she was also invisible.

II.

HER MOTHER GAVE HER A NAME ONE MIGHT GIVE A princess. Genevieve. Her brother, Renald, called his sister princess. He was three years older. He used to sleep in the living room, while Genevieve shared the bedroom with their mother. After Renald left, he told her the living room was hers, all hers, not just the corner with the stacked books.

Queens sometimes lost wars. Genevieve's mother lost a custody battle. Renald's father got his life in order and ordered the queen to relinquish their son. The queen wasn't afraid of the courts. She wasn't afraid to fight. Even so, the queen had no ammunition. No proof other than feeding, clothing, and providing shelter for her son that she was good for him. My son needs me, she told the judge. *I'm his mother*, she decreed. The queen didn't know that even titles can be shredded like crowns of folded paper.

Renald's father won and took him away. When the queen lost, Genevieve could see victory on her brother's face, his eyes twinkling like Christmas had arrived early. Genevieve never saw him glow blue, but he glowed with joy that day. When the queen tried to hug her son good-bye, he recoiled, pushing her away.

"I'm going to win you back," the queen said simply, limply. Her smell of cigarette smoke reached both Genevieve and Renald's noses. He turned his nose up at the queen.

"No, you won't," he said.

The queen didn't bother to reprimand. She raised her hand to her son's face. He turned around and walked to the front door. Renald stood by the door and waited. He didn't pack any belongings. He didn't need reminders.

"Not taking your figures?" Genevieve asked him.

Renald glanced at his toy figurines sitting idly by the couch. "My father already bought me brand-new ones. He told me to leave everything here."

Genevieve nodded. "When will you be back?"

Renald's answer was a shrug. He walked over to her and hugged her. Genevieve cried.

After Renald left, the queen noticed her daughter's eyes, red and watery. She ordered her daughter to dry her eyes and read. Then the queen went to the bedroom and closed the door. Genevieve heard her mother's sobs through the closed door, sounding like wails from blades slicing skin.

The next day was Genevieve's birthday. No happy birthdays sung. The cake with the blue icing sang *I'm sorry* instead. Her brother was the only friend Genevieve had, the queen knew.

As Genevieve listened to the queen crying her blues, she grabbed one of her picture books, one of many about a princess being saved. She read the words aloud slowly, sounding out each word to get its meaning, ignoring the blue light on her skin. She already missed her brother.

Her half-brother, who half-belonged to the queen's kingdom, who was whisked away to the other kingdom he half-belonged to.

Who knew a prince would have been saved instead of a princess?

ON THE EVE OF GENEVIEVE'S EIGHTEENTH BIRTHDAY, the queen commanded her to go the library. The queen needed to conduct business, and her princess could not be present. The queen presented her with a backpack.

It was a new one, new to Genevieve, but it looked old and worn. It was red. And heavy. Genevieve asked the queen a question with her eyes. This wasn't her backpack, not the one she used for school.

"Don't look inside," the queen said. "Wait until you get to the library. Look then. Look alone."

Genevieve nodded and placed the backpack around her shoulders. The queen gave her a hug.

"Be light," she said to her daughter, her hands holding her shoulders. "Don't ever cower to *nobody*. You got power. Live like you want."

The queen turned her around, pushing and rushing her out, snipping, "Go, go, get out!"

Genevieve glowed. Her body shone in blue. She pretended that the light shining on her meant something more. Maybe it was her cloak of courage. She faced the queen.

"Mama," she said. Then Genevieve asked her a question she always thought to ask for years but never did. Answers were all around her, but there always seemed to be one answer she couldn't see, an answer she couldn't know unless her mother told her.

"What's going on with you?"

The queen was silenced. During those several quiet moments, the princess studied her mother's face and frame. Her sunken eyes, her drunken demeanor. Her arms, lanky, lifeless but still muscled. Her weakness and strength. Her despair and beauty.

Genevieve then studied the distance between them. Her queen had often been kind to her live-in subject but kept a distance. Kept her busy with reading. Lots of it. School was Genevieve's only business, the queen ensured that. No need to be nosy about something if there is no purpose behind it, the queen had often told her when the princess was curious about her mother's business, asking questions. Focus on your books, the queen had always ordered.

So Genevieve treated her schooling like a business. One she owned. An entrepreneur of her studies. Her product was excellent grades, her distribution was time, her price was any kind of social life, no sacrifice. No parties, no friends, no one else to hang with but her mother. And they didn't even hang. The queen was all about her business. Genevieve was all about hers.

There was a fork. She would soon go away to college—the queen ensured that as well—but the heaviness of the red backpack felt like she was not leaving for the afternoon and early evening. Their paths would no longer travel together. Genevieve felt that in her gut.

The princess stepped closer to the queen and softly yet sternly repeated her question.

The queen answered her daughter's question with a command.

"Get out!"

Genevieve shook her head. "No," she said.

Tears falling down the queen's face, she slapped her daughter's own. "I call the shots here, my home. *Mine.* You don't belong here."

Genevieve's blue light faded.

"You never saw me. The others didn't see me either, but I never cared about them. Just you and Renny. You both never saw me," she stuttered.

Genevieve turned around and reached the door. She opened it and left.

GENEVIEVE EXITED THE APARTMENT COMPLEX AND walked down the street, bypassing running kids and a few elderly women. Her neighborhood was full that August day. The heat brought people outside. Fire hydrants released water, gushing into the streets to jubilant children. An ice cream truck played a jingle. Billy Ocean blasted from one car radio, while RUN-DMC blasted from another.

The end of summer was near. The heat felt like a cape, making Genevieve's red backpack heavier. She reached the library and went inside. Only a few people were there, two librarians and an old man sitting by himself staring into space by a far corner.

Genevieve headed to a shelf with books about history. She grabbed a large tome on World War II and sat by a small table close to the shelf, taking off her backpack and resting it on the floor.

Before she opened it, a young man only a few years

older than Genevieve sat down across from her. She recognized him. One of the queen's minions.

"Word is that your mother's shutting down her business—all of it."

"My mother's business is not my own," Genevieve said.

"I'm not supposed to say shit to you about it, but everybody's talking."

"I don't enjoy talking much," she said. "If you could leave and let me enjoy my time, I'd appreciate that."

"He's coming for her. She owes him money. He's bringing his men with him."

The queen's business partner. Genevieve ingested the information, resting her hand on the book.

"Just tipping you, that's all. I work for her no longer. I'm switching trades. Going legal. If anyone asks you, you don't know me."

"I don't know you," Genevieve verified, placing her other hand on the book. "Now leave."

He stood up and walked away quickly, leaving the library. When Genevieve confirmed his departure with her eyes, she grabbed the red backpack and looked around, seeing no one within eyeshot of her. She unzipped the backpack. Bundles of hundred-dollar bills wrapped with rubber bands. A folded piece of paper. She took it out and unfolded it.

Keep reading. Keep moving.

Genevieve returned the note to the backpack and zipped it up. She left the book on the table when she stood up and sped herself out of the library. Once she emerged from there, she ran. She ran seven blocks back to the apartment complex.

She stopped running when she reached the street across from the complex. There were police cars and an ambulance. A huddle of people gathered, watching the commotion.

Bodies rolled up in black plastic rolled out. She saw a couple of people turn their heads and witness her standing across the street. They shook their heads. No one walked across the street to console her.

She knew. The queen was dead. What she didn't know was that her mother fought. She called the police to report a murder before it was committed. She used an old recorder to tape the conversation between herself and her business partner. Got him to confirm bad business they both conducted together. She struck him and his men with a sword shaped like a pistol. Then she struck herself.

All Genevieve knew was her mother was gone and she left a gift. Not the money. The note. Her last instructions. Genevieve accepted them as love. It would be hard for her to accept love from anyone else. That's what Genevieve would become—hard.

But not stagnant. She would keep moving.

She glowed, smoldering so bright that if people could have seen her shine, they would have been blinded. She cried and shimmered and moved forward.

IV.

THE FORMER PRINCESS FOUND LOVE. OR BETTER stated, love found her, then pursued her. In 1995, love in the shape of a man a few years older than her who asked her if she would have coffee with him after a business meeting. He was a medical professor serving as an expert witness in a case she worked on. She was the only woman of color at her firm, an assumption the man made as an icebreaker.

"I'm the only one too," he said after first meeting her. "In my department. But it feels like I'm the only one on the entire campus. Can you relate?"

Of course she could. She attended a college where she was the only Black woman in all her classes. Where she was told that she was accepted only because she was Black. Where people who didn't look like her looked at her as if she was in the wrong room. She fended off comments and assumptions like a warrior, fueling and guarding herself with her mother's passed-on strength. She replied to repulsive remarks with stinging wit, her sharp retorts continuing well into law school, where she was also one of the few students of color.

In both places she felt out of place, not only because of the color of her skin or how often it glowed blue. She thought she didn't belong because she found herself uninterested in anything other than the books in front of her, beside her, on the back of her inside her backpack, all the knowledge inside her.

So she could relate—but only by so much. She didn't date. She made no friends. Though some people tried. She denied all of them, the opportunistic ones and the well-meaning ones. She would deny her expert witness. She would try.

She told him she couldn't socialize with him for professional reasons. He suggested that they could when the case was over.

She rebuffed him. Months later, he showed up at her office saying he had to meet with her regarding business, making it his business to get to know her.

She was no longer a princess. She no longer wanted a prince. She was a conqueror belonging to no other kingdom than her own person.

Her refusals didn't deter him.

She tried the truth. Nothing fended off suitors like insanity.

"I glow blue now and then," she said. "I don't know why, but I do. No one can see it but me. It doesn't scare me and doesn't confuse me anymore. Do you still want to take me out?"

"I do," he answered. "You're glowing now. You've shined all the times I've seen you."

He was correct, but he didn't know how. Genevieve was glowing. Blue and bright.

She understood what he meant. His sincerity overwhelming her reluctance, she said, "You may pick me up at seven."

He did. They went out for pizza. Then they went out. She surprised herself. She let someone in. Not just anyone. A good man. An earnest one. She married him.

She still reserved herself. To everyone outside her new family, she remained the same—serious, solemn.

She gave her new family—her husband—her heart comprising of her time, her body, her ears, her words. He gave her back tenfold.

Years later, her family expanded to include twin daughters. She named one of them after her mother. She felt like a rebel raising them, rebelling against herself. Marrying her husband was her first betrayal. Having and raising their daughters decimated her isolation. Her daughters became the new queens of her new kingdom. Even though Genevieve had the most say in taking care of them, her girls were the ones who ruled.

She watched them closely to see if any of them would glow the same color, if at all. To see if her uniqueness had transferred. For the three years of their lives, she saw a different kind of shine. A glow of gratitude. Her own.

A FIRE BURNED DOWN HER LIFE. SHE WAS AWAY ON A case. Her husband and daughters did not survive. Genevieve felt like she wouldn't either.

She tried. The words from her mother's note came

to her mind, but they were no longer powerful. She no longer cared to read, no longer felt the need to keep moving.

She spent mornings, afternoons, and evenings sitting in front of her burned-down home. Neighbors sympathized. They brought her food and blankets. They offered their homes, where she could regroup. She entered their homes only to use the bathroom. She returned to the outside of her home to sit and stare.

Until several days later, when her body glowed blue again.

"Get off me!"

She scratched and swatted herself. Then she stood, continuing to slap her body. It was the early morning before the sun had risen. The sky was dark. All she could see was her blue light.

"Get off me!"

Never had she yelled before, but she did. Lights in nearby homes turned on, and a few neighbors came outside. She ran, almost as fast as she did when she ran to her mother, running to save her. She ran through her neighborhood until she reached the nearby beach. Her blue light continued to shine. The glow became brighter when she reached the ocean. She ran into the waves. She swam into the water, but her light didn't wash off. It became so bright she could no longer see her own body. She stilled her arms and legs. She let herself sink into the ocean. She didn't hold her breath. She would let the water in.

THE WATER DIDN'T GO IN. HER LIGHT BARRED IT. IT only felt like water rushed into her body. The light left, but she couldn't see it. She lost consciousness.

GENEVIEVE WOKE UP AND FOUND HERSELF IN A BRIGHT room. The shiny gray walls almost looked like silver. A thin rectangular mirror hung on one wall next to a closed door that almost looked invisible to the rest of the room. She wore a long blue hospital gown. She lay on a table with bars of metal constraining her.

She didn't feel constrained. The metal felt like paper. Her body glowed blue.

A man walked in. A full head of brown hair and brown eyes, he wore a black suit, sharp and tailored, the kind of suit she recognized from her old law firm, implying he was well-funded.

He stood by the table. "Genevieve. How are you feeling?"

She didn't answer.

"I'm sorry for your loss."

"I'm not here for my loss," Genevieve noted. "What do you want from me?"

"You're not going to ask me who I am or how I know your name or what happened to you first?"

"No."

He nodded slowly. "Goodness. You truly don't care what happened to you. Or what may happen to you."

She didn't. Not caring could make anyone feel calm. She looked away and up.

"You should be threatening me now," the man said. "Your life could currently be in danger, and you don't seem to mind."

She continued to look up, keeping herself still.

"You lost everything but gained something extraordinary. Your body is glowing blue right now, isn't it?"

Genevieve looked at him.

"I can't see it, but I know it's there. You wouldn't have survived your jaunt into the Atlantic without your powers."

She raised her eyebrows.

"I know who you are," he said. "Genevieve Purpose Gryson. Thirty-five years old. Born in the Bronx. Graduated summa cum laude with a bachelor's degree in history. Graduated summa cum laude from law school. Worked for Juniper, Thornton and Sands for several years, turned down a partnership offer twice."

She continued to stare at him.

"I will skip what I know about your family. Again, I am sorry for your loss."

Genevieve said nothing.

"You're strong enough to remove your constraints. You could leave here anytime. I want to make an offer to you before you do."

"Where are we?"

"In the basement level of a building. Washington, D.C."

Her body still glowing, her body newly knowing, Genevieve's arms and legs bolstered with strength. She lifted her limbs, and the metal constraints fell to the floor. She sat up on the table. The man looked unfazed.

So did she. She detected something. The sensation was new. Heightened awareness. She became aware of emotions and contemplations of the stranger before her.

She became aware of herself. She could snap the man's neck and leave.

"You want to use me," she said.

"Yes," he confirmed. "On behalf of the organization I work for."

Genevieve couldn't tell the man what she wouldn't confirm to herself. She didn't want to wake up. She detected she couldn't put herself in a forever sleep even if she tried. Her blue glow would not allow her. Her glow would always keep her alive.

"You can do a lot of good," the man continued.

"I've already done a lot of good."

"Yes. Your pro bono legal work with homeless families. I'm referring to a worldwide kind of usefulness."

"Before I consider your offer, tell me what all of this is," Genevieve ordered the man. "Before doing so, please bring me appropriate clothes to wear. Pants, a silk blouse, and flats would suffice. Size eight, medium, and size nine, respectively."

The man placed his hands behind his back. "I don't work for you," he said.

"You *will* provide what I requested. If I'm going to

consider your business proposal, I will be wearing appropriate clothing."

"We're not a business," he said.

"Irrelevant," she countered.

He slowly nodded and left the room.

She stared into the mirror but didn't see her own reflection. She saw through the mirror to the man speaking to an older woman with short red hair wearing a gray pantsuit and oversized eyeglasses. She saw the woman nodding her head at what he communicated. They both left the other room.

Genevieve waited. She thought about her husband and children. How she missed them. How stranded she was.

Even though she felt empty, her muscles felt full. She couldn't ignore how hard her limbs became. How hard she would become again.

THE MAN RETURNED AN HOUR LATER WITH TWO shopping bags.

"Leave the bags on the ground," Genevieve said.

The man followed her command.

"If you try anything on me or any of my colleagues," the man said, walking closer to her, "you will be stopped."

Genevieve detected he was lying. She couldn't be stopped.

"You already know that if I wanted to hurt you or your colleague, I would have by now. Please leave. I will be ready to listen to what you have to say in five minutes."

The man failed at keeping a poker face before he left. Genevieve looked through the mirror and saw him leave the other room. She walked over to the bags and inspected them. She removed her hospital gown and got dressed. She smoothed her hair back and down with her hands.

She looked through the mirror. A door in the other room opened. Both the man and woman with the over-sized glasses stepped in. They looked at Genevieve. She couldn't detect them through the walls. She waited.

They entered the room. They formally introduced themselves. Then they presented their offer. A job that would pay handsomely.

Genevieve warned that if they tried to restrain her against her will again, she would restrain them instead and pain would be involved. Then she asked for more information. They gave it to her. She requested a seven-figure salary over their previous six-figure offer. They agreed. She didn't need to mull it over. The glowing wasn't going to leave her, and neither would her powers. She'd tried to do something to rid herself of herself and failed.

There must have been a reason. A purpose.

V.

MORE LEARNING. TRAINING. FIGHTING.

Genevieve kept reading. Not books. Files. Folder after folder on domestic and international criminals of interest. She was assigned missions. No partners, she asserted. She didn't care to have them at her old law firm job, and she wouldn't have them now. All she needed was information, tools, and time.

Her first objective above all was to identify anyone who glowed just like her. The woman with the oversized glasses told her she was currently the only living person she knew who glowed blue. She detected she was telling the truth.

For years since her childhood, she'd wondered what that would be like—finding someone who shined like she did. Would she feel connected? Not by choice but by force? Like family?

She completed missions. In the span of two years, she saved lives on every continent except Antarctica. She protected people. She took people out. Kept notes. Mental ones.

She was all about her business. She had nothing left in her life other than that.

Until her jaunt into the Bronx. There she saw a light.

THE LIGHT WAS BRIGHT. SHE DROVE ON A ROAD AND saw a blue light shine in the middle of a huddle of people standing on a corner. After stopping at a traffic light, she utilized one of her powers. She forwarded her vision yards in front of her and saw a baby being wrapped with a blanket.

The baby was also wrapped with light. Neon blue.

What shocked Genevieve more—that she had finally found another blue light or that it emanated from a baby?

Neither.

Her sentiment stunned her. She hadn't felt this way the numerous times she saved lives, when she saw the grateful faces of the women, men, and children she stopped from being slaughtered by oppressors. Not even when she saw toddlers who resembled her own daughters.

The light shined brighter. A paramedic held the baby. There was no one around she could assess as the baby's mother. A man held soiled newspapers she deduced were the baby's previous blankets. He must have been the man who found her, she speculated.

She took mental notes. The time. How many people stood around the baby. The names of the street corners.

The facts she collected faded back into sentiment. She pulled the car over to a metered spot and waited. She would follow the ambulance that would carry the baby to a hospital. She would shadow the paramedics and then the doctors and nurses who would examine her. She would take her time in deciding whether or not she would inform the organization about the baby.

She would sit in the car, sit with her emotion, one she never knew she could have again. More powerful than her powers.

Belonging.

Genevieve glowed. She gleamed the same color as the beaming baby. No one noticed either of their lights. Once she remembered her invisibility—*their* invisibility—she remembered her pain.

She wanted to drive over to that corner and claim the baby as hers. She wanted to say to everyone there that she didn't give birth to the baby and had no legal nor family ties but even so, the baby was still hers. She wanted to convince the bystanders that she would care for the baby for the rest of her life. The baby would not grow up alone, and Genevieve would not die alone—they both would be there for each other. They would always see each other shine.

Genevieve scolded herself. She had the will but no longer the strength—the kind of might that could have convinced her to care for the baby the way she cared for her daughters. They were gone, and she was done.

She would no longer rebel against herself. She would remain her own ruler. She would follow her own decree.

Genevieve would continue to collect data. She would notify the organization about the baby. She would become the baby's safeguard, her guide. Maybe her mentor. Never her mother.

As she shut her blue light off, she conquered her empathy, banishing it to never return.

Her Mother,
Nneka

CHIOMA SAT IN HER KITCHEN BLOWING UP BALLOON AFTER BALLOON. PURPLE. HER FAVORITE COLOR. SHE LOOKED AT THE BALloons spread about her kitchen counter. After she tied another balloon filled with her air, one of her accomplishments fell off the counter and lightly bounced off their tiled floor.

Her sons ran into the kitchen and saw the purple balloon on the ground. Matthew, her oldest son (by five minutes), kicked the balloon first. Paul, her slightly younger son, tried to copy Matthew but missed the balloon and kicked air instead.

Chioma slapped her hand on the counter.

"Stop it!"

They stopped kicking. They didn't look at her and didn't need to. Her voice was enough. They returned to the living room. Kenechukwu, Chioma's husband, smiled from the other side of the counter where he sat, reading the *New York Times*.

Chioma glanced at him, catching his smile, almost matching it with one of her own. Her smile, no matter how happy, was always reserved. No full up-curve of her lips, rarely did she show her flawlessly aligned teeth when she showed joy or satisfaction. Just a small lift of the corners of her mouth. Those small lifts were regularly present around her husband. Her husband's common sense and practicality made her swoon daily. The man of her dreams was the man with no dreams, just goals and achievements.

"Darling," Chioma said. "My balloons are falling. My air is not enough to make them rise."

"Flying balloons are overrated," Ken said, flipping a page. "You already know that you need helium to make them rise."

"I know. I was hoping that my breath would be enough. Perhaps I should command them to fly."

Chioma saw her husband smile again—she'd made a joke. A halfhearted one, but a joke nevertheless. Chioma was not one to make light of much, but she knew the day would be heavy.

That day, her half-sister turned twenty-five. That day, her half-sister would be forced to prepare herself to live a life of her own. Chioma, her husband, and their children were leaving for Nigeria the following day. Leaving to live there permanently. Chioma would finally return home—a home that didn't belong to her half-sister.

Chioma hoped that a birthday party would serve as just that—a birthday party. Instead, it would be a farewell celebration. Chioma was excited to leave White Plains, New York, with her family. She was happy to leave the house she'd tried to claim as her own for years. The guilt of leaving her half-sister behind didn't overpower her elation. The guilt of not feeling guilty enough propelled Chioma to throw her half-sister a party. A party that her husband found impractical.

"My love," he coaxed, staring at more purple balloons finding their way to the floor. "We should give her money instead. If your goal is to make her feel cared for, this party will not succeed. Only our friends will be here this evening. She has no friends attending this party simply because she does not have friends. The sting of that will be felt, I am certain."

Chioma looked at her husband. "That is unkind," she said.

"And accurate," he added.

Chioma pushed away the remaining balloons from the counter and watched them fall.

"I apologize," Ken said. "I am wrong."

Chioma nodded her head. "That was unpleasant of you."

"No, I did not mean wrong as in mean, I meant wrong as in mistaken. Your sister has friends—they are just not the kind who would make the effort to support her. You are an excellent sister, but you are not her comrade. She will need friends."

"She will need family."

Chioma's clarification silenced them both. They knew they were the only family she had. The next day, her sister would no longer have that family around. Chioma refused to take blame for that. The liability of her half-sister's loneliness belonged to their father, Demetrius, who was dead. It wasn't his dying that caused her sister to be alone. It was their father's decision to have another child with a woman who wasn't Chioma's mother. The woman who abandoned her daughter—Chioma's half-sister—soon after she was born.

"Regarding her lack of people, you are correct," Chioma conceded. "Though I must try. This is the right thing to do."

"We both know there can be a difference between propriety and caution," Ken said. "In this case, my love, I vote for the latter."

"I wish she would find a husband already," Chioma snapped. She removed herself from her kitchen stool to gather the balloons.

"I will call that party center from the boys' birthday last year," Ken said. He folded up his newspaper and took out his cell phone. "I will order purple balloons with strings. They will rise high."

Chioma's lips lifted a degree. "What about your vote?"

"If we are going to do something impractical, we might as well implement it practically."

Sense. Chioma sighed. "Thank you."

HER MOTHER AND FATHER HAD MOVED TO THE UNITed States when Chioma was five. Demetrius got a teaching job in New York, and although Chioma's mother didn't want to leave Nigeria, she didn't want her husband to leave her and their daughter either. Chioma's father promised to send her mother money from the States, but her mother knew living apart would have created a corridor for her husband to look for someone else.

Turned out her mother getting sick instead gave him the space and a corrupt certificate to couple with someone else.

Her mother got sick when Chioma was eight years old and died soon afterward. Her mother must have loved her husband for reasons that didn't make sense, Chioma often thought. Her father was dense, she believed. The man left her mother for a woman who had no direction. No direction other than the front door of their house. The front door she entered after Chioma's mother died, and the same front door she opened to leave Demetrius soon after Chioma's half-sister was born. He named the baby Colleen after the woman he claimed was his soul mate.

"You must have no soul," Chioma said once to her father when she was a teenager. She said this to him when he wasn't looking. She whispered it to the view of his back when he talked across the hallway to his younger daughter about her mother, referring to her mother as his soul mate, saying Colleen was born from love even though her mother was nowhere to be seen. Obioma—Colleen's middle name and the only name by which Chioma called her—was five years old when she asked her father who her mother was.

"Soul mate, your mother was that to me. She still is."

Chioma called her father soulless once more from her room, whispered it again when she would have preferred to write it down on a piece of paper and tape it to the front door of his house. Chioma visited him and her half-sister in the States during some holidays from Lagos, where she lived with her Aunty Grace and where she attended school. Her mother's sister had no daughters and loved Chioma as her own. She never made Chioma feel like a leftover, never made her feel overlooked. Aunty Grace was Chioma's saving grace, as her aunt kept her connected to her mother's relatives, who ensured she stayed in contact with her extended family. She kept Chioma a part of their collective, kept Chioma collecting memories with her mother's people.

Chioma couldn't accomplish the same with Obioma. Obioma was Chioma's people, but Chioma's people were not Obioma's people. Chioma's cousins, aunts, and uncles never acknowledged Obioma as one of them. Mainly because she wasn't a part of them. She was Demetrius's daughter, a reminder of his betrayal.

Maybe that's why Chioma never called Obioma by her first name. Chioma didn't like her sister's first name, mainly because she didn't like the woman who bore it, who bore a daughter of the same name, who bore the badge of home wrecker.

Chioma knew better. Her father's soulless soul mate didn't wreck anything. Obioma's mother couldn't destroy a home that was never constructed. The foundation was gelatin, melting away with her father's girl-friend's presence. Chioma's mother was someone to cook for him, someone to clean for him, someone to be there just to be there, not someone for him to cherish. Her father didn't love her mother, Chioma judged. He didn't love his wife enough to keep his soulless self away from his soul mate.

"Your mother is a useless woman," Chioma told Obioma over the years. She sometimes said it clinically—there is a ground, the earth is round, your mother is useless. "If she ever comes back to you, you will recognize her and see how she would be a waste of time to you."

Obioma looked hurt each time Chioma shared her tidbit. Chioma would offer as a salve: "I wish my mother was your mother. If we shared the same mother, you would have known what it is like to be cared for."

After their father died, Chioma tried to treat her half-sister with more consideration. It was easier to offer kindness to her younger sister after Chioma married Ken. After Chioma and Ken moved into Demetrius's house, it was simple to treat her half-sister like her own daughter. Chioma and Ken were in charge. They brought in the money with their respective careers of law and medicine. They paid the bills.

A few years after Chioma and Ken had their twin sons, they decided to move to Nigeria. After the decision was finalized, Chioma wondered how Obioma would fare without them. Obioma was on the cusp of twenty-five. That's what Ken reminded Chioma after she asked her husband, "What about my sister? What will she do?"

EIGHT YEARS AGO, WHEN THEIR FATHER DIED, CHI-oma was in upstate New York, attending her last year of law school. Her flip-up cell phone buzzed while she was at the library. She glanced at her phone and saw the word "House." It must have been her father calling her for some random reason, she thought. Maybe he was going to ask her if she would be returning for Thanksgiving. She had already made plans to go to her best friend Lynne's home for the holiday.

She ignored it. She had thirty more pages to read and more cases to review. She would call back at her leisure.

After a few minutes, her phone buzzed again. She ignored it again, looking back at her pages and note-book. Her cell phone buzzed again. She snatched her phone and turned it off. Nothing would keep her from her studies.

An hour later, she finished her reading and gathered her items. She drove back to her studio apartment. She fixed herself a bowl of chicken soup and sat down on the chair next to her fold-up table. She took out her phone from her pocket and turned it back on. She had three missed calls and one voicemail. She listened to the voicemail message.

"Chioma. I called 911, and some people are here to help because…Dad died. He died. He's dead…" A small hiccup and sniffle. Then a click.

Chioma closed her phone and softly rested it next to her bowl. She ingested portions of soup, slowly and neatly. That's what her mother had taught her when she was a girl. She needed to finish her food before attending to anything else. She prioritized her mother's training.

After Chioma finished her soup, she grabbed her phone and flipped it open. She dialed the house's land-line. She heard the answering machine. She heard her father's voice say: "Please leave a message. Afterward, read a book. Thank you."

"Obioma. This is Chioma. Pick up the phone. Now."

Obioma answered.

"Stop crying. Tell me what occurred."

Through brief intervals of sobbing, Obioma told her. Chioma took out a pad and paper and wrote down notes. After Obioma finished her summary and Chioma finished jotting down the information, she instructed her half-sister to stay put until she arrived. Obioma said okay and hung up.

When Chioma shut her phone, she took her pad and reviewed her notes. Then she washed, dried, and placed her empty bowl in a cupboard in her kitchenette. Then she packed an overnight bag with impeccably pressed clothes. She gathered her other needed items. Within minutes, she was ready to leave her studio and walk to her car. Before she left her apartment, she opened her phone again and dialed the house.

"Chioma?"

"Everything will be fine. I am calling to tell you that. The world has not ended. Your life will keep going, and my life will as well. For the next four or five hours, keep that as your reminder until I get there, *biko*."

"What does *biko* mean?" Obioma asked.

Chioma shut her phone. The man didn't teach her any Igbo. Chioma shook her head as she asked herself: How could he have not taught his daughter any Igbo?

Chioma kept shaking her head until tears ran down her face. She dropped her bag to the ground and bowed her head. She said a prayer for her sister, crying throughout.

Chioma thought to say a prayer after her husband left the house to get the flying balloons. Before he left, he ensured their sons took their naps and reassured his wife that he would return with rising purple balloons. She believed him. It was easy for her to believe him because he treated promises like purposes, goals like guarantees. Those purple balloons would rise high in their house soon enough, anchored by strings, a perfect balance between going up and staying down, swaying yet staying grounded. She thought about her sister.

"Obi will need a steady income," she said to herself,

staring at the pieces of the purple balloons she popped. She placed the squiggly shards of rubber on the counter as if she would somehow soon use them for another project. Though she knew they were useless, she wasn't ready to throw them away.

She recognized the uselessness of her own thoughts. To think about what her half-sister needed was not helpful because ultimately Chioma couldn't provide most of those things. Obi will need to go steady with someone, Chioma thought. She will need everything steady. Their house was a good start, had good bones, was a good investment, but it wouldn't be good enough, Chioma assessed.

Her sister would need more. She would need aspiration, ambition, an aim, something to work toward, something to look forward to, someone to lift her up, someone to keep her grounded. Someone who simply would be around.

Both Chioma and Ken were correct. She would need family and friends. A network of reliable people. Thinking of her father's passing, Chioma glanced at her cell phone sitting on the left side of the balloon shards.

That's what Obi will need, Chioma thought—her sister would need a new, updated cell phone. Her half-sister was disconnected from technology the same way she was disconnected from her own Igbo heritage. A landline wouldn't be enough. Chioma opened her flip phone and called her husband.

He answered instantly. "My love."

"While you are out, would you go to one of those network shops and purchase a new cell phone? It will be my gift to Obioma."

"Birthday gift or farewell gift?"

"Both."

"Would you like to purchase two presents instead? One for her birthday and one to say good-bye?"

"It would be more efficient to get one and have it count as both," Chioma replied.

"I agree, much more sensible," Ken said.

"I thought about what you suggested earlier. Perhaps giving her money would be better than this charade."

"Charade?"

"This will be a party for us, I have realized," Chioma said.

Ken said nothing.

"I thought it would be more efficient to also have our friends come over so we can properly say good-bye to them," Chioma added. "I do not know why I am feeling like this."

"Feeling how?"

"Conflicted," Chioma answered, staring at the balloon shards.

"That is normal," Ken assured. "My parents felt similarly after we all found our spouses and left their house. They were both elated and downcast. Change causes more change and sometimes creates an avalanche."

"Do you feel this way as well?"

"No," Ken replied. "We are moving and things are

changing, yes, but you are my constant. If you and our sons are there, all will be well with me."

Chioma sat up straight on the stool and grabbed the popped balloon pieces. She threw them away in the trash can, leaving her counter clear.

"Thank you, darling. Thank you."

"I will be home shortly."

Chioma shut her flip phone and left it on her counter. She looked at it as if the phone answered all her questions. Obioma would call her, Chioma figured. If she needed anything, she could reach Chioma from anywhere. Instead of the landline, a new cell phone would be her sister's lifeline, and if her sister needed any of her friends, a cab, to order in food, she would have an updated phone. That, and some money, would do it. She couldn't teach her sister how to swim, but she could leave those as rafts. Her half-sister would have those until she could teach herself how to stay afloat or maybe even swim somewhere.

Chioma smiled a rare smile, a full one, finally feeling free to get work done.

CHIOMA AND KEN'S FRIENDS AND GUESTS ARRIVED on time. Helium-filled purple balloons floated close to the ceiling. The catered food Chioma ordered was presentable and delicious.

Obioma was nowhere to be found. Chioma detested lateness but hated no-shows more.

This would not have been embarrassing if not for the birthday cake Chioma had also ordered, the birthday cake made with chocolate and caramel. Chocolate and caramel were Chioma's favorite dessert flavors. She knew Obioma liked the flavors as well, even though she didn't know Obioma's favorite desserts. She didn't know her half-sister's favorite anything.

After their guests left later that evening, Chioma and Ken packed up their photos showcasing both sides of their families, showing all the faces of immediate and extended family members except for three. No pictures of Demetrius, no pictures of Obioma, and certainly no pictures of Obioma's mother—the greatest no-show Chioma knew would never show anywhere in her home, except through the likeness of Obioma.

She wondered where her half-sister was but was not worried. She felt relief from the observation—if she wasn't worried that evening, she most likely wouldn't be worried about her sister living a hemisphere away on a day-to-day basis.

Chioma realized she didn't have any pictures of her half-sister to hang up on the wall in her new home. She also realized she never planned to have any images of her sister in her new home in Nigeria. She wondered what she should have made of that—surely, she loved Obioma.

Yes, she did, caring about her sister was her obligation. Chioma felt shame when she made another realization. Her shame came from her certainty—if she and Obioma shared the same mother, Chioma would have loved her half-sister much more.

CHIOMA AND KEN WENT TO BED SOON AFTER THEY cleared the kitchen and packed away more of their belongings. Their twin boys woke them up in the morning by jumping on their bed. Chioma was ready to chide them, but sentiment stopped her. Their last morning in their house in the States would be happy. She slightly smiled. She looked over at Ken, who looked at their boys the same way, idly amused by their jumping fits of joy.

Chioma and Ken were diligent about their days, starting them by swiftly rising out of their respective parts of their bed and marching to their morning rituals. That morning, they sat on their bed and watched their sons jump from the bed onto the ground. Their sons ran around the room.

"Do we have the energy to stop them from running?" Chioma asked Ken.

"I will make us coffee," he replied.

After Ken left their room, Chioma asked her sons, "Shall we see if your Aunty Obi has returned from wherever she went yesterday?"

The boys ran from the room, but instead of running into Obioma's room, they ran downstairs to follow their father. Chioma stood up and put on her slippers. She walked out of her room and across the hall to Obioma's room. The door was slightly ajar. There was just enough space for Chioma to open the door farther and look in. She saw her sister sleeping soundly. She shut the door all the way quietly. She smelled a hint of coffee. She looked around the hallway and then again at her sister's closed door. She would drink a cup of coffee downstairs first. Then she would return upstairs again. Most likely Ken would accompany her, and Chioma would check to see if Obioma was still sleeping. If she was still asleep, Chioma would make breakfast and then wake her sister after the food was prepared.

Perhaps that would be the last time she would prepare any kind of food for her sister, Chioma thought. She didn't foresee herself visiting Obioma at the house in the future, and she didn't think Obioma would visit her in Nigeria. That thought didn't make Chioma sad.

Their lives would move forward with each other by phone but without each other in person. That was the way, Chioma knew. That way would not be sentimental but even better. It would be efficient.

CHIOMA WASN'T PREPARED TO SAY GOOD-BYE TO HER mother, Nneka. Her father brought her to the hospital and told her that her mother would soon depart from the world. They stood outside of the room where Nneka laid lifeless but still alive. Chioma searched her father's eyes for tears or any kind of sadness. She found no signs on his face. He looked impatient. Like he just wanted his wife to move on so his life could move on already.

"I do not want to say good-bye," Chioma said. "I want to pray."

"Prayers will not help your mommy now. I am sorry," her father said. "Please, go and talk to her. Tell her good-bye before the beeping stops. When the beeping stops, she will be gone. I do not want you to have regrets later."

"What are regrets, Daddy?"

"They are something you do not want to have but will, if you do not say a proper good-bye. Please, go now and say it."

Chioma followed her father's orders and walked inside the room. Chioma's father closed the door shut from outside.

"Mommy," Chioma started. "I do not want to say good-bye."

Refusing to look at her mother again, Chioma left the room. Her mother died twenty minutes later. Chioma understood what her father meant years later after he died. She did have regrets. Not for not saying good-bye but for failing to say I love you. Chioma often found those three words trite when said together, but maybe her mother would have woken up if she'd said them.

She didn't regret not saying good-bye to her father. She regretted not telling him that he made a mistake.

Obioma's mother might have been Demetrius's soul

mate in theory, but surely not in practice. Maybe he already knew he had made a mistake falling in love with a woman who would eventually leave him and their daughter. Maybe that was his last thought before he passed away—his true love who truly wasn't there for him.

Chioma remembered the last conversation they had, one week before he passed away. They had their weekly phone chat, and he updated Chioma on Obioma's starting her senior year in high school. How Obioma would soon be applying to colleges. How Demetrius wanted his younger daughter to follow his older one, to excel in her studies just like her older sister.

"I know you will guide Colleen. You will always be there to support her."

Chioma was ready to tell her father no. Chioma would not always be there, because she would live a life of her own, that Obioma's mother was still alive somewhere and she could show up and be their daughter's guide instead.

"Ask her mother," Chioma almost said. "Find your soul mate and ask her to be your daughter's role model."

Chioma instead said, "Of course, Daddy. I will help her."

LOOKING AT OBIOMA'S FACE, CHIOMA CHOSE TO NOT say good-bye. Chioma told her sister that she would start depositing five hundred dollars a month to help her with bills. Making sure her sister would fare well without her was the most efficient farewell, a most dutiful departure.

They stood on the porch outside of the house. The cab waited with Ken standing nearby holding one of the doors open. The boys were settled in the backseat.

Chioma told her sister what she knew to be true.

"I love you," she said, smiling a full smile, her rare one without reservations. The three words she said had reservations of their own. She loved her sister, but only by so much. There was a line, a solid boundary that Chioma didn't tell. She thought, sadly and solemnly, that Obioma could tell.

Chioma didn't love her sister more than her husband and sons. She didn't love her sister more than her mother, Nneka. The love Chioma had for her sister was unconditional yet quantifiable. The disgrace Chioma felt from that truth didn't disappear. It stayed like the house would, sturdy and secure, the concrete of their circumstances keeping it still. Chioma hoped she would leave that shame behind her, that maybe she would see it fade in the rearview mirror of the cab.

Obioma told her that she'd bought a one-way ticket to Nigeria. She told her that she would eventually sell the house and she could live with them there.

Chioma's smile disappeared, her shame staying. She told Obioma that it was not a smart idea, and that they would discuss it later.

"Call me," were Chioma's parting words. She turned

around and joined her family. After they were all settled inside the cab shaped like a van, it drove away.

Chioma looked at the rearview mirror intently until both her sister and the house disappeared. She felt expelled from the house, an exile from her own ruling, her guilt like a gift she couldn't give back, her love for her sister both efficient and permanent, yet permanently unavailing.

AUTHOR'S
ACKNOWLEDGMENTS

I AM GRATEFUL TO EVERYONE WHO HELPED ME TO nourish these stories and to flourish as a writer.

To my parents, thank you for all you have done for me. I am and will always be grateful for the sacrifices you made for me.

To Vanessa Willoughby, thank you for accepting my collection into your Kindred series and for your spectacular editing and wonderful guidance. You will always have my gratitude for opening the door and leading the way.

To the amazing publishers Mary Ann Rivers and Ruthie Knox, thank you for the marvelous organization that is Brain Mill Press. Thank you and the Brain Mill Press team for the copyedits, promotion, and all your exceptional work with preparing this collection to be published. Thank you for publishing my collection and for your unwavering support. Your commitment to inclusive storytelling is inspirational.

To Felicia Penza, thank you for your brilliant and beautiful work on this collection's cover.

To the editors of journals and magazines who have previously published my work, thank you: *Blue Lake Review* ("Bars"), *Carve Magazine* ("Demetrius"), *Black-*

berry: A Magazine ("True, Perfect"), *TINGE Magazine* ("Speakers & Headphones"), *Jabberwock Review* ("Proposed"), *PANK* ("Text Me a Photo"), Auburn Avenue ("Paying"), *Day One*, and *The Brooklyn Quarterly*.

To Darin, my partner in life and in love, thank you for your amazing support and encouragement. Your smile is my sunlight.

To all my friends, relatives, mentors, colleagues, and readers who helped me by providing encouragement, feedback, and insightful critiques over the years, I say heartily, *thank you.*

ABOUT THE AUTHOR

KEM JOY UKWU'S FICTION HAS APPEARED IN *PANK*, *BLACKBERRY: A magazine*, *Carve*, *TINGE*, *Blue Lake Review*, *Jabberwock Review*, *Auburn Avenue*, *The Brooklyn Quarterly*, and *Day One*. The manuscript version of Locked Gray / Linked Blue was named as a finalist for the 2016 New American Fiction Prize. Born and raised in the Bronx, she currently lives in New Jersey with her husband. More of her work can be found at kemjoyukwu.com.

CPSIA information can be obtained
at www.ICGtesting.com
Printed in the USA
LVHW02s2002050218
565348LV00014B/1431/P

9 781942 083979